John Lowry's Blues

A Novel

By

Seth Turman

Tully House Press
Minneapolis

First Edition. Published by Tully House Press, Minneapolis.

The following is a work of fiction. The people and places occupying its pages are either products of the author's dramatic imagination, or are used fictitiously. Any resemblance to real events or locales or persons, living or dead, is entirely coincidental.

Acknowledgements: The author would like to thank James Wagner, Jessica Armbruster, Lucas Rayala, and Emily Schmalz, without whom this book would not have been possible. He would also like to thank his wife and all of his family, as well as his sixth grade teacher, Mrs. Gail Totino.

ISBN: 9780615932293
LCCN: 2014933514

For Jeff

JOHN LOWRY'S BLUES

1

The late afternoon sunlight bounced under the one open shade in the otherwise poorly lit room and landed right on John Lowry's face. If he'd been at home and felt more comfortable, he might have closed his eyes and sat there, feeling the soft glow against his skin. But he was nervous because Mello's marijuana was taking a long time to get there, and he was almost running late for work. If he was late picking up clients again, Carl said he was canned. And he was only helping Mello out as a favor. He got some free smoke out of it, but it wasn't worth his job. He shifted himself in the recliner so the glare wouldn't obstruct his view of the two fools on the couch, their baggy clothes making them look like a couple of enormous deflated balloons. They sat slack-jawed and unconcerned, their stoned eyes following their videogame character's exploits with the cold detachment of a child burning his last ant in the sun.

John was feeling old, but if being young meant you were one of these blobs, he didn't see much hope and figured he was good right where he was. Their music was terrible. It was some rap song about H to the Hizzy, or Wheezey, God knows what. He didn't get it. It was somebody called Rawhide, according to one of the blobs. His character on the television dragged a woman out of her car, and then beat her with a baseball bat. Blood spattered onto the street, pixilated in bright, day-glow red. The kid and his friend sat stone-faced. He punched his controller with lazy precision, a trail of smoke rising away from the blunt that rested in his lips. John wondered what the object of the game was, or if there was a point system of some sort. Instead he asked, "You guys play this game a lot?"

"Yeah, all the time," one of them answered, after a long pause. He wasn't sure which. He had looked down at his watch for a moment. It was just as well. The boy's character hopped into the hijacked car and started to drive. John took the sirens as an indication that the police were chasing him.

The other kid pulled the blunt out of his friend's mouth and started to puff. He blew airy, weak smoke rings, his mouth opening and closing like a goldfish. He offered the blunt to John. "No thanks," He said. "Don't have the wind that I used to." Sadly, it was true. At sixty-five, he just didn't anymore. But he still had a toke once in awhile, although he wouldn't be caught dead smoking with these yoyos. He liked to sit on his front porch at dusk and watch the sun go down, glowing pink and orange and silhouetting the crooked New Mexico horizon. He'd roll a joint and sip his Jim Beam whiskey until it warmed his belly and the landscape cooled and the sun was almost gone. When he felt sufficiently hazy he would wander back inside and watch an old movie or two, the kind where the violence took place off-screen and relied on the viewer's imagination. He liked that. Kids today didn't have to imagine anything. They were spoon-fed violence like Fruit Loops.

He looked at his watch again. He didn't know what the hell was taking Brad so long with the quarter pound. Mello had obviously forgotten to mention the part about having it ready and waiting. The minutes were passing, and Raw-Hyde kept pounding out of the speakers. None of the words he rhymed even made sense. The fools on the couch kept their eyes on the screen. Every time John came to pick up Mello's weed for him, there was a different pair of guys sitting around playing video games and getting high, and they all looked the same.

With the rare exception of a few songs he had heard Mello playing on his stereo, John hated rap. When he was young he had enjoyed black culture, but it seemed different then. There were boundaries being expanded, and rules being broken. He had been a pretty big R&B fan, and he liked Ray Charles a lot. Chuck Berry was great. Some of his high school friends had turned him on to Thelonious Monk and Charlie Parker. These guys seemed like innovators to him, even geniuses. But the rappers? They were asinine. Now they were breaking rules, but they weren't replacing it with anything worthwhile. It was bullshit, and poorly rhymed at that. Mello told him he just didn't understand, but John didn't think so. He wasn't behind the times that much. He could still recognize quality, and this wasn't it. But it wasn't all rap's fault, or the blacks. It was everything. Hell, it was more the white's fault, if you really wanted to get down to it. Their spoiled kids were the main ones funding all this crap.

John had been waiting for fifteen minutes. He had to drive around a bachelor party tonight, and needed to get moving if he was going to make it, since he was picking them up on the other side of town. The Las Cruces Limo driving gig was a good job. He'd been with them for over a year, and intended on keeping it that way.

John lit a smoke and looked across the cluttered coffee table for an extra ashtray. He found one, an overflowing plastic salsa container with melted edges. A few stray butts fell and rolled onto the floor as he maneuvered it closer, through a maze of Taco Bell wrappers and empty soda cups.

"Thought you don't smoke no more," one of the kids said.

"This is different."

"How?"

"I don't know."

The kid looked at him. He went back to hitting the blunt, and his friend backhanded him in the shoulder.

"Gimme that shit. You already hit it, bitch."

"Whatever. You're playin' the game, man."

"You guys think Brad might be coming back soon?" John asked.

"How should I know? I'm not his keeper," one said.

"He just went around the block. Can't keep it here no more. Five-oh's been creepin' lately," the other explained.

"Ok. Great," John said. That was all he had. He took a long drag from his cigarette. He coughed, a deep cloacal wheeze, his chest and lungs tightening as if a giant had squeezed him. It didn't stop. Before it reached a point of extreme awkwardness for everyone, he decided to get up. He walked down a narrow, dark hallway to the bathroom. He leaned against the counter. A few moments went by and his fit calmed down. He spat in the sink. A small circle of blood sat in the middle of his phlegm like an egg yolk. That wasn't so bad. Last week was worse. Maybe he wouldn't need to go to the doctor.

Then he looked at the hand he covered his mouth with. It was covered in little red dots. He turned the knob on the sink and quickly washed it away and glanced at his watch. He was going to have to leave soon, with or without Mello's reefer. He walked back down the hall to the living room.

"Here you go." John turned his head and saw Brad standing behind him. He had a shirt on with the word Hoobastank printed across it. "Sorry about the wait. Had to come in the back way. Can't be too careful." He tossed John a brick of weed and plopped onto the couch.

"It's ok. I used to do this myself when I was your age." John stuffed the brick into a black Adidas bag. He snubbed out his smoke in the ashtray, trying not to let any more butts fall.

Brad mumbled something to him about telling Mello to give him a call. John nodded as he left. He didn't bid his two friends on the couch goodbye. They were busy. One was in a part of the game where he was banging a prostitute in the back of a car. The other looked on, perma-stoned. Blaring out of the speakers now was one of Mello's personal favorite masters of linguistics, as he called them, Little Skittle. John had actually heard of him, somehow. He figured it was probably because he was white, which pissed him off, but he wasn't quite sure why.

As he walked away from the house he could still hear Little Skittle carrying on about how good he was at rapping. He crossed the street and walked a few houses down, to where his limo was parked. It was ten to six. Not too bad. He lit another smoke and started the car. When he looked in the rearview mirror to pull out he saw a light flash.

His pulse kicked. He prayed it was nothing. The light flashed again and it turned right onto the street and came screaming to a halt behind him. It was an unmarked car. He knew then what was happening, but as if to prove it beyond all supposing, suddenly there were more cars and lights pulling out from an alley, then from the road in front of him. His foot instinctively hit the brakes as the car in front came charging down upon him. He let off the pedal and put his hands on the dashboard. He was pretty sure they weren't planning on shooting him, but their zealous entrance persuaded him not to take any chances.

A man's voice behind a bullhorn told him to step out of the car. He did as he was told. He dropped his cigarette and put his hands above his head. He saw that the police were in the house arresting Brad and his moronic friends. How could he possibly have had the luck to be here right before a raid? This was Mello's fate, not his. John wouldn't even have been there if Mello wasn't so lazy.

Someone made him drop to his knees hard. He asked them what the hell was wrong with them.

"This one's got a mouth on him." He pushed John forward into the street, and dug his elbow into the back of his neck. He felt like a large man. "You gonna give us problems, buddy?"

"No problems, chief." He felt gravel sticking to his face.

2

Jail was crowded and stank. At about two in the morning, three drunk Mexicans got dumped in the communal cell and the youngest of them puked all over himself and his area of the floor, causing his compadres to abandon him. The other two tried to piss in the open toilet and largely missed, prompting a huge good old boy from west Texas to start carrying on about the wave of dirty, illegal immigrants infecting the nation like a sickness, taking away jobs from good, hard working folks like himself, and a scuffle ensued. The big fellow wildly threw around the Mexicans, though they sustained no visible injuries, until the guard came and told everyone to settle down, or he'd settle it for them.

John was going to be out of a job. His boss already didn't like him because he was old and slow. And he was late sometimes. And he blamed John when that crazy old bat rear-ended him at the bowling alley.

It would be hard to find new work in this economy. This was bad luck.

He placed his hand on the cold metal bench beneath him until it cooled his skin, and then covered his black eye with his palm to try and relieve some of the pain and swelling. It didn't do much for the swelling, but it felt good. The arresting officer who had thrown him to the ground had been Native American, and didn't appreciate being called chief. He had let John know this by handcuffing him, standing him up straight, and punching him out. After waking up in the back of a squad car, John had contemplated telling the guy that he hadn't meant anything by it, but decided not to. Once a cop or guard started to get physical, it was like a light switch was flipped. It made it that much easier for them to do it again, and talking to them never worked. It only made them angrier.

About an hour after his fight, the Texan sidled over to John and struck up a mostly one sided conversation, which detailed most of his life up to that point, including intimate details about his four ex-wives, and his criminal history, which included petty larceny and meth dealing. He concluded with the fact that he was currently being held for robbing a convenience store.

"And you're worried about these vaqueros taking your job?" John finally asked, thumbing at the Mexicans, who were now sulking in a corner, looking like they were planning the Texan's death. "Ten to one they work legit jobs."

"What? The Texan looked confused. "No, man, it's a social issue I'm talking about, here. The future of our nation. Our children. It's bigger than you or me."

"Can you sit somewhere else?"

"What?"

"Ever here the expression, you know, people in glass houses..." John immediately worried that he was going to be attacked, but at the same time he welcomed it. Maybe he could break this big lout's nose before he knew what hit him. It could be fun to focus his anger on something immediate. But the Texan only stared at him as if he'd been insulted at a state dinner, over caviar and fine cheese.

"What are you, a preacher?"

"Yes."

The Texan grumbled something about the nigger-loving preacher and sat in the opposite corner from the Mexicans. He continued a conversation back and forth with himself for about twenty minutes.

John was arraigned later that morning. His public defender said he had a good chance at getting the charges reduced, since Officer Brian Redstone couldn't keep his hands to himself, and he would try to work that angle. He took a couple of polaroids of John's eye. With any luck he might end up with a fine and probation, maybe community service. Worst case would be a few months in jail.

John had called his friend Aubrey Gillis the night before to see if he could get the limo out of the impound lot and bring it by Las Cruces, and pick up his van from there. Aubrey ran a repair shop out of his gas station and had a tow truck. John also asked him to run by his house and feed his cats, and call a bail bondsman, but only if it wasn't too much trouble.

In what must have been the late afternoon by John's reckoning, though it was hard to tell because there were no clocks or windows in the cell, the guard came and called out, "John Lowry?" John nodded, but the man wasn't looking at him. He looked like he was texting someone on his cell phone. "You made bail."

The sun was shining outside. John got in Aubrey's truck and turned around to see Aubrey's two sons, Clay and Adam, sitting in the back. "What'd you bring them for?"

"Bonnie's at church group."

"So you brought them to bail me out of jail? They're kids, Aubrey."

"They don't know where they are," Aubrey said, pulling out of the parking lot.

John turned around again. Adam, who was two and in his car seat, covered his face up. Clayton, the four year old, stared back at him and smiled. "Do you know where you are?" John asked.

"We're at jail," Clay said, bashfully.

"See?"

"They thought they were at the hospital till you said jail." Aubrey scratched his beard and checked the rearview mirror before getting on the highway. "Anyway, you should be glad to have such a fine welcoming committee as these lads to greet you after your incarceration. Right, guys?"

"Yeah!" Clay yelled.

Adam's response was slightly delayed, but then he chimed in, "Yeah!" as well.

The ride home was silent after that except for the radio, which Aubrey fiddled with whenever it changed to something he didn't like. Adam fell asleep after a few minutes, and John and Clay stared out the windows.

They followed Historic Route sixty-six until they reached Entierro's outer limits, which was pretty much most of the town, and then turned southeast on Robin St., right in front of The Next Wave Garage and Filling Station, which Aubrey owned. Behind it they passed a junkyard full of rusted-out cars, V-8 Fords and Chevy Impalas, cars so old and weathered you couldn't even tell what they used to be, their tires burrowed halfway into the earth like boulders. Bullet holes numbered in the thousands, despite the chain link fence Aubrey's father had put up in the seventies. Weeds and prickly-pear cacti flourished in spring bloom all around, adorning the hollow machines with small splotches of purple, yellow and red.

They went two more blocks and passed a small graveyard with a bent and decrepit iron rod fence, and

16

pulled up to John's tiny house about six-thirty. His red, white, and blue striped van was sitting in the driveway.

John nodded and opened the truck's squeaky door, trying not to wake the kids. Then he thought better, leaned into the truck, and whispered, "Thanks. Tell Bonnie sorry for the trouble." He motioned his head toward the boys. Clay was starting to squirm.

"No worries," Aubrey whispered back. "Try and get some sleep. Stop by the shop for some cards tomorrow."

"Better not invite me. I'll clean you out to pay for my legal fees. Oh, and speaking of which, I'll pay you back for getting my van out tomorrow."

"Whenever, John. No rush."

"I'll do it tomorrow." John patted the seat cushion in a neighborly fashion and shut the door. As Aubrey backed out of the driveway he turned and clumped up the steps of his porch.

Pirouette, John's calico, rubbed against his leg affectionately as soon as he opened the door. He patted her on the head. She was definitely the lover of the two. Merlin, the moody shithead, didn't like anyone except John, and even then only about half the time. He would frequently attack without warning, especially if he felt neglected. John scanned the living room's perimeter for his orange tabby, ready to deflect a possible assault, but saw Merlin safely asleep on the windowsill. He gave Pirouette a scratch on the back, and picked up the pile of mail Aubrey had left on the floor and brought it to the kitchen. He opened the pantry door and poured food into the cats' dishes, waking Merlin. He charged into the room with a loud cry, and promptly began to inhale his dinner.

John pulled a beer out of the fridge, put it against his eye and went into the bathroom. He cracked it, took a big frothy swig, and lit a smoke. He put the beer down on the sink and looked at his eye, the smoke dangling from his lips. It didn't look as bad as it felt. Only a thin veil of yellow and blue surrounded the swollen part. He laid his cigarette in the ashtray on top of the toilet and ran his fingers over his moustache, trying to see if it had any more gray than when he had left the house yesterday. Didn't look like it. He briefly examined the thinning area on the back of his head with a small hand mirror. It wasn't balding, only thinning. He took off his shirt and squeezed his pecks together to see if they were still defined at all, and, not satisfied, did ten pushups lengthwise on the bathroom floor. He didn't start coughing, which was good, but it did shorten his breath more than he would have liked. He definitely wasn't as strong as he used to be. Then he looked at the floor more closely and realized it was slanted, which probably made his pushups a little harder. He briefly fantasized about kicking Mello's ass the next time he saw him. The lazy bum could get his own weed next time. If he could find someone new to sell it to him.

The beer was no longer cold enough to feel good on his eye, so he slammed it on his way out to the living room and grabbed a new one from the fridge. He started water on the stove for some mac and cheese, extinguished his cigarette under the faucet, and threw it in the garbage.

He sat on the plaid couch in the living room and watched the news while he ate, now fairly buzzed from the beer and whiskey he had just poured. The first news story was about a lady in New Jersey who had killed a woman who was eight months pregnant by slicing her open with an exacto-knife while she was still alive and taking the baby out of her so that she could keep it as her own. The two had met each other, oddly enough, in the visiting room of a prison where they were seeing different people. They struck up a friendly conversation, and the next week went to hang out at the offender's apartment, where she had tied her up and killed her. She was caught because she had brought the baby to a hospital for care, claiming she had just had it, and the staff thought she seemed suspicious. She had served three years in the early nineties for stealing a baby from a supermarket checkout line and had been released. John changed channels.

It was another news story. This one was about a man on a Greyhound bus in Missouri who had, for no apparent reason, turned to the passenger next to him and began stabbing him with a large, serrated knife. Witnesses who were sitting in front of them said no words were exchanged between the two prior to the attack, and he seemed totally calm, like a robot, as he stabbed the screaming man to death. The bus was stopped, everyone ran off, and when the bus driver and a trucker who had stopped to see what was going on went back on the bus, they found him knelt over the dead man in the aisle, decapitating him with his knife. He chased them off the bus and went back to the body, calmly bringing the severed head to show off through the glass doors. He was charged with second-degree murder. John turned off the television just as a blurb came on about three soldiers dying in a roadside blast. The room was dark.

These things would not stop happening, and he didn't understand why, even after all he'd seen. He sat for a long time and stared at a tiny glare on the screen of the television, and let his thoughts consume him until he thought he was might scream and smash everything in his house, and shatter his own skull to bits with a hammer.

To clear his head he got up and started washing dishes. It went surprisingly well. When he was finished he went through the mail, separating the bills from the things he wanted, which wasn't much. He set aside a National Geographic magazine that Aubrey had brought over, about animal minds and vocabularies. It had a picture of a happy looking sheep dog on its cover. A letter addressed to him in what appeared to be a woman's handwriting

19

stuck out from the rest of the junk mail. The return address was in Minnesota. He leaned against the counter, feeling eerily as if another presence had invaded his kitchen. The writing seemed familiar. It was from a Caroline Fischer. The only Caroline he knew was his baby sister, whom he hadn't seen in at least twenty years. He opened it quickly and pulled out a letter that was several pages, and began to read. After a moment he quit reading and shut his eyes. He slid to the floor and held the letter tightly in his hands, which were shaking, and leaned over and began to cry. Merlin chose this moment to violently attack his leg, and John had to swat him away.

3

As Laura Trout drove to work, a sappy love song on the radio reminded her that John stood her up the night before. Though she hadn't called to see if anything happened, she knew nothing had, other than one of his mood swings and maybe a card game with the guys, and she was for damn sure his moodiness had made a fool of her for the last time. She had watched part of *The Bridge on the River Kwai* and ate her lemon chicken and rice pilaf alone, before deciding his choice of a movie was not what she considered entertainment, and she put in *Romancing the Stone*. John was a bore, anyway, she told herself, and only slightly better than her vibrator in bed, although at his age she was lucky he could even get it up, and she decided she was too old to be flopping around like a tramp with some rascal. So even though she liked him, she was happy to push him out of her mind like she had so many others over the years, and she was surprised by how easy it still was. She was still her own woman. If she saw him today, she would just tell him it wasn't working out. He could deal with it. She turned up the radio. A song about strength, happiness, and sunshine was playing. She thought it might be Sheryl Crow. The heated blacktop glistened from the morning rain, and her red Dodge Durango spewed water from the tread of the tires as she drove west toward Entierro. She had the front windows down, and the mineral smell of wet rock surrounding her was refreshing.

Entierro, population five hundred and fifty-five, had the look and feel of a town that had been scooped up by a giant and ground between its palms, the remains falling to settle into the dust along New Mexico's eastern stretch of old Route sixty-six. This wasn't to say there were never any visitors. Now being a historic piece of American folklore, people did sightseeing across all that was left of it, even if there wasn't much in some places. Travelers in cars, motorcycles, and motor homes cruised through the old dying artery somewhat infrequently now, due to rising fuel costs, sputtering like the last bit of blood keeping it alive.

Laura had built herself a decent life here, although it wasn't easy. She purchased an old rundown diner about fifteen years before and reopened it to become one of the main roadside attractions on this stretch of the old highway. She called it Laura's. Folks called it Laura's Diner. It had a neon sign, a jukebox that played oldies and some modern country and rock for the kids, black and white checkered floors, built-in swivel stools at the bar with faux red leather tops, gingham table cloths, and orders were taken and sent to the kitchen on paper. They served ice cream sundaes, malts, burgers, steak, chicken fried steak, and breakfast all day.

It was ten a.m. when Laura got to work. Piper was clearing tables with Eduardo, the bus boy. Piper's hair was pink today and in a ponytail. It bounced as she skirted from table to table, overloading her arms with dishes. It looked like a busy morning. A few customers were still eating, mostly truckers and a couple of families. Aubrey's weird friend Mello was sitting at the low-bar, stuffing his face with pancakes.

"Much better," Laura said, following Piper into the kitchen.

"Huh?" Piper looked confused, unloading her arms' cargo into the dish pit.

"Than green. Although pink's still a little much, honey."

"Oh." Piper turned around and put her hands on her hips, playfully. "I liked the green hair! The green hair was good! It was like green eggs and hair!"

"I like you blonde. You're natural color is so cute. And classic."

Piper put her hand up in mock defiance. "Whatever, lady." She practically ran back to the dining room. Laura grabbed an apron from the cabinet and tied it on. Piper was a classic beauty. She just didn't seem to know it, which Laura adored. She would always get embarrassed when Laura told her. Maybe it was the word itself that was the problem: classic. Young people had strange aversions to certain words for no reason these days. She remembered Piper saying once, "Don't say classic, Laura." Maybe she thought it was dorky. So she would find a new way to say it. That might help.

Laura looked at the morning's receipts before doing anything else. There were almost seven hundred dollars in sales, which was a great morning for her little diner. She was about to go out to the dining room to help Piper and Eduardo because there wasn't another server on until noon, when she heard a scratching sound at the back door.

"Piper!" She called though the swinging door.

"Huh?" Piper stuck her head in.

"Did you feed Martin today?" Martin was a stray dog who had shown up one day several years prior, who loved people, but would never let anyone take him inside. No one knew where he went at night, or how survived the winter cold.

"Aw shit. I forgot." She made a wincing face.

"Pi-per! You've gotta remember to feed him when I'm not here early." Laura walked over to the back door and popped open the large plastic tub of dog food.

"Sorry, Laura. I… was a little late."

"You can still feed him if you're late. Why were you late?"

"I just was."

"There's a reason for everything. What'd you forget your knickers and have to go home and get 'em?"

"My what?"

Laura opened the back door and dumped Martin's food into his dish. He dug in frantically before it all hit the bowl. Food spilled on his head and rolled everywhere. His tail wagged like a dirty mop. Laura looked into the distance and saw John walking from down the street. She slammed the door closed. Piper looked at her.

"You'll see," Laura said, sliding the large dead bolt to its locked position. "So did you have a date last night?" she asked.

"What?"

"Is that why you were late?"

"Yeah."

"Better not have been that Bud boy. He's no good, honey. Thought you got rid of him."

"I did."

"Then who was it?"

"Just…" Someone knocked on the door and Piper jumped.

"Someone new? Oh, honey, good for you! Who is it?"

"Just a boy…"

"I know it's a boy, honey." The knock came again, louder.

"Laura! Hello?" John's voice called from the other side. "I saw you! C'mon, let me in."

"Who's that?"

"Another mutt looking for a handout."

"Are you gonna let him in?" Piper asked.

Laura sighed. "Yes. Better let me take this, honey." Piper nodded and went up front. She turned around before going through the swinging door and Laura shooed her on. Laura slid the lock and opened the door. "This better be quick, I'm busy."

John walked meekly into the back of the diner, but something was wrong. He was limping and had a black eye. He looked terrible, in fact, but she could tell he'd taken great care with his appearance. His hair was combed and slicked over neatly, and his shirt was ironed and tucked in. His boots even looked polished.

"Hey, listen, I'm sorry," he began.

"What happened to you?" She cut him off, her initial anger fading, and she reached out and put her arm around him. "Come here and sit down." She motioned to a stool.

"I'm ok. I'll stand." He did stand, but awkwardly, still uncomfortable around the opposite sex. They'd been dating a few months. Some men never got over it, she supposed. "I tripped over Martin this morning and twisted my ankle," he explained, looking shyly at the floor.

"How did you do that?"

"He was sleeping in my doorway. Fell over him when I left. He does it all the time, but sometimes I forget." He seemed to think for a moment and then added, "I don't know why he sleeps there. I don't feed him. I like him well enough, but when I trip over him I get mad and kick at him. I'm surprised he still comes around."

"Well, you shouldn't kick him. He's a sweetie."

"I've only connected once or twice."

"How did you hurt your eye?"

"I got arrested and an Indian cop took offense to something I said and punched me."

Laura stared at him for a moment to make sure he wasn't kidding. Then she burst out laughing. John was saying, "…didn't mean anything, I didn't even see he was Indian…why are you laughing?"

"Is that why you missed our date? Because you were in jail?"

"Yes," he said, smiling. "Well, yes, and no. I wasn't in jail last night. Aubrey bailed me out yesterday. I just didn't think about our date because I was so tired and out of it. I didn't get a wink of sleep in jail. There was this crack dealer, or crank…are they the same thing? …and these Mexicans."

"What did you get arrested for?"

"I went to pick up some weed for Carmello- you know he gives me some for free if I do it- and the place got raided. But it may not be that bad, because…"

"You mean Mello, Aubrey's goofy friend?"

"Yup."

"He's eating breakfast up front." She immediately wished she hadn't given out this bit of information. John's face changed.

"Really?" he asked, moving towards the front of the store.

"Where are you going?"

"Just wanna talk to him."

"John, don't go talk to him right now if you're angry."

"Ok." He didn't stop.

"No, listen to me. This is my place. Don't go starting any trouble." This wasn't working. He just kept limping

26

forward, like a hunchback. He was too old to fight. Was that what he was going to do?

"It's ok. No trouble."

"John, I mean it."

"Ok." He pushed open the swinging door, limped into the open kitchen, and rounded the corner of the low-bar with surprising efficiency. She followed and stopped at the counter, seething.

Mello was bent over his plate, soaking up the last drops of maple syrup and melted butter with a huge bite of pancake jammed onto the end of his fork, his long hair hanging down around his head in greasy strands. Just as John approached him he looked up, his mouth agape, which only made his extreme overbite look all the more pronounced and strange, and he said, "John?" just before John grabbed him by the head and slammed him face first into his empty plate.

"Benny." Laura said, trying to get her cook's attention, but Benny was already dropping his spatula onto the flat-grill and trying to get around the bar. People turned and jumped in their seats, and the dining room hushed.

Mello said, "Hummwhaah?" as his face came up out of the plate, sticky and cringing, his eyes squinting from the syrup, his nose red and mashed in. John shoved him backwards out of his chair, but as he did he lost his balance and fell over Mello's chair, on top of him, and the two hit the floor in a tangled mess. Laura followed Benny around the counter and saw them rolling over each other, Mello now kicking wildly like an animal scratching its hind legs at the belly of its opponent, and he got the upper hand on John, got on top of him and started to punch him in the face with flailing arms, and then he put his hands around John's throat, and squeezed, and John reached up and did the same, and Mello hissed, "Stop it!" as blood dripped out of his swollen nose. John just squeezed harder, it looked like, because Mello tensed and bore down on him, the veins popping out of his sinewy arms as he choked the old man below him. John's face was red and puffy. Laura worried that Mello might kill him. She went to the stove and grabbed a clean pan by its handle, but couldn't decide who to hit or what to do.

Benny and Eduardo were trying to yank Mello off of John, but they ended up on the floor. It took longer than Laura expected to get them apart, and more chairs were knocked over. Benny held John down, who was still trying to get up, but was coughing and wheezing now, uncontrollably. Eduardo had Mello across the room now, but Mello wasn't trying to get any closer, he was just yelling at John, "You're fucking crazy!" and looked almost in tears. John finally stopped moving. He patted Benny on the arm gently until he let go. Then he rolled over on his hands and knees and coughed grotesquely, as if he were shifting great tectonic plates with his hacking. He did this for a long time. The room slowly started to regroup.

Eduardo ushered Carmello out the back of the establishment, and as they went past her, Laura told him not to worry about the bill today. He nodded, his hand covering his nose, blood still oozing between his fingers. "Thokay," he said. She decided to follow them and grabbed some towels, making him wash himself with the hose out back by the dumpster.

"I'm tharry, I don' know whad happend," he said, looking at her apologetically between strands of bloody, syrupy, hair.

"I don't either," she said. "I know it's not your fault, but you'd better just not come around for a little bit. Maybe a week or two. Alright?"

He nodded, looking down. He blew his nose. The sound almost made her gag.

"Maybe you should go to the hospital."

"No inthurance," he said, shaking his head.

"I think is broken," Eduardo said, looking at Laura, concerned.

"Yeah, we're gonna call the ambulance. Just to be sure you're ok." She nodded to Eduardo. He pulled out his cell phone.

"No, I hade hospidals. I hade them. I'm fine. Really."

"It might need to be reset."

"No, really. I'll justh take thum more towels." He grabbed a clean towel from Eduardo, and to their surprise, started to run away at a light jog.

"Mello. Wait, honey."

"Come on, you need your nose fixed," Eduardo said after him, and started dialing, but Laura put her arm on his. She shook her head and shrugged. They watched as Mello jogged out of view. When they went back inside, John was gone.

4

He wasn't tough anymore. He kept thinking this over and over until it became like a parasite eating his mind. How had he let a gawky bastard like Carmello Bencini beat him in a fight? Had the old man finally settled into his bones for good? Had he lost his edge? If only he hadn't tripped over that chair. His ankle was the problem. It gave out when he put his weight on it. And he was about to position himself to knee Mello in the crotch when Benny and that busboy broke it up. That could have gotten him loose. John played it over in his head, trying to figure out how he had lost, what he could have done differently, but he kept coming back to the indelible reality. He just wasn't the same anymore. His face didn't look like this last year. Getting up every morning was getting increasingly painful.

He held an ice pack up to the fresh lump on his head and watched a special on meerkats on one of the animal channels. He nursed a whiskey. Merlin made a running leap at the television whenever the meerkats did a lot of chattering. Pirouette slept with her head nudged between his leg and the couch.

Laura didn't want to see him again. After he left the diner without saying anything, it took him all day to work up the courage to call her. First she hung up. After a couple of calls she was finally willing to talk to him, but it didn't do any good. She had made up her mind earlier that morning, apparently, but didn't have a chance to tell him. His behavior regarding Mello had only solidified it. He was a little fuzzy from the whiskey he had begun drinking and was having a hard time mounting a sufficient defense. At first he thought it had sharpened him, but soon enough he was stammering and tripping backwards over his words, unable to recover any modicum of suaveness. But that did not deter him, and Laura was soon reduced to saying things like, "You're too old for me, anyway." Did she really mean that? Or was she just placating him because he was pathetic and drunk? He hated being placated by a woman. It depressed the hell out of him.

"What'd you mean? How old are you?" he tried not to slur.

There was silence on the other end of the line. Then, "Fifty-two, John. You know that. I'm not seeing you again, no matter how old you are. I shouldn't have said that."

"Well see, that's only what, thirteen years? Wait, what month were you born?" He hated math.

"I'm going now. You take care of yourself." She sounded like she was going to cry. Was it out of pity or something else? Or was he just imagining it?

"I'm not going to start siphoning off the nursing homes just yet, missy. I got a few more years of chasing hot young tail left in me." There was no response on the other end. No laughter. No soft crying. "Hello? Laura?" She had hung up.

The first fight John ever got in he lost. In the eighth grade, Leroy Fontaine and Greg Masterfield beat him up after school. He couldn't remember why anymore, which bothered him. He didn't like forgetting things, even though he was used to it. It didn't matter anyway. With those two idiots, it could have been anything. He had gotten some good licks in, but wasn't very big for his age, and they sent him packing. He probably weighed a hundred and five pounds soaking wet. When he got home, his old man was pissed. He was filthy and his new shirt was ruined. After he got reamed, John walked upstairs and passed his little sister, Caroline, on the top step.

"Are you okay, Johnny?" she asked, or something, in her small voice. He didn't answer. He just went into his room and shut the door. He wished now he had told her something, anything. Just because she looked so scared.

Caroline's letter said the old man died in nineteen eighty-five from lung cancer. That was over ten years after he last saw him, or any of his family, for that matter. She was remarried now, she said. She found John through some sort of internet site that searched for loved ones.

He couldn't think of anything he would have wanted to say to his father, but hearing of his death filled John with a nameless dread that he just could not shake. What was it? Loneliness? Some perverse need for closure? The old man had been gone for over twenty years. John had spent all of those years feeling bitter about a dead person. He didn't even know if that was a waste. All he knew was that it made him angry.

John switched from meercats to The Simpsons, and then the news, which he quickly turned off before it got ugly. He pulled his .357 out from under a pile of flannel shirts in his closet. It was loaded. He sat on the couch and put the cold barrel up to his temple. It felt alien and calculating, precise and vulgar in its cold touch. He put it between his teeth. He thought of the mess it would make on the wall behind him, and chuckled inwardly. A small thud from outside the front door made him jump. He held the gun behind his back, opened it and found Martin staring at him. He whined. John shut the door and hid the gun under the couch cushion. He grabbed a handful of cat treats from the kitchen and threw them out the front door, onto the porch.

Bored, he looked through his pot box and found an old roach in the bottom. He lit it and inhaled the musty smoke. He coughed a little and puffed a few more times. He lay on the couch and his head felt like a lead balloon. He propped his feet up and rubbed their arches on the couch arm, wishing he had a masseuse. He shut his eyes. Drifting to sleep, he dreamt a vision of Uncle Sam skinny and dying, his old coat and top hat caked with the dust and mud and…was it blood?...of what John knew to be countless years of war, and he held out his hands to John's, and said, "I'm sick. Help me," but the voice was his father's. John took his hands in his and they crumbled away the moment he touched them, ash withering between his fingers, scattering from a savage and hostile wind, and his face did the same, and the whole body shrunk and caved in on itself, the clothes collapsing into a pile on the floor. But something small was moving around in the fabric, trying to escape, and when it's head popped out it was a baby. It jumped out of the pile of clothes and scampered around in circles, screaming, "Whooohoo!" like Homer Simpson, pumping its little fist in the air as if it had hit a home run, and it ran up to John and leaped weightlessly through the air like a basketball star and gave him a high five, and when John awoke with a start he was soaked with cold sweat and his heart was booming.

5

The first was an old woman in Saigon, nineteen sixty-four, about the middle of his first tour. John was a few months in, pushing paper behind a desk, and already decided that he wanted to be in the bush. This wasn't what he signed up for. Processing paperwork for officers was boring and though the city was exotic and strange, it's novelties were quickly waning. He wanted to be where the fun was. His next tour would be with the infantry. It was already settled.

The only reason he was even carrying a weapon was because Bubbles, this staff sergeant he'd bought a couple of grams of hash from, got into it with a local gang member. John was out at a bar with Bert Lancome and a private he knew only as Exly when he saw the little hustler pull a knife on Bubbles. They weren't in a serviceman-friendly place. It was dirty and local. Fun. He had noticed Bubbles standing at the bar, but didn't wave or acknowledge him because he looked like he was there for business, and John was young and green and wasn't sure about etiquette. He was pretty sure he did the right thing by not saying anything when the drug dealer came up to Bubbles and started shoving him and yelling at him. Bubbles was playing it cool, and seemed to be telling him he'd take care of it, pay him back, but the kid wasn't having it. He wanted reparation then and there. He pulled out a knife, and John grabbed their bottle of booze off the table and walked up behind him, smacking him square in the back with it, right between his skinny shoulder blades. It was a heavy bottle and didn't break. It made a dull snapping noise, and the guy dropped the knife and fell forward into Bubbles, who set him up, and knocked him straight down with a punch to the jaw. Bubbles was a big guy, who had done some boxing in college. The dealer got up and left, but not before he looked John over real well, and he pointed at the two of them and spat some vile sounding rhetoric that sounded to John like a promise for vengeance. Bubbles told him not to worry, but that he might want to carry his issued .45 for a while, just in case.

John eventually found out from other people that the drug dealer had a sister who was a whore, and Bubbles had beat the shit out of her so bad that she couldn't work for weeks, and afterwards she incurred a permanent limp. Bubbles was apparently a real sadist, and had done this several times, according to various sources, but this time he just happened to do it to a girl whose brother was dangerous. Bubbles eventually got stabbed several times in an alleyway and somehow lived, but John never saw him again.

Two months later John was still carrying his gun. He had just returned a care package from his father, unopened, and was feeling guilty about it, and debating if perhaps he shouldn't try and go get it back, maybe pay the postal officer to go find it for him. He was walking the streets aimlessly, soaking up his feelings and trying to catalogue them in some sort of rational way. He was lonely that day. Not really for home, but for something, an intangible, and he thought about going to one of the brothels, which he hadn't done yet, but decided against it, worrying that he too might end up stabbed or dead.

As he was passing the Joint United States Public Affairs Office's press center, near the Rex Hotel, he smiled at an old woman carrying a basket. She had a purple scarf around her head, like a bonnet. She smiled back at him as they passed each other and reached in her basket. A few seconds later, an explosion rocked the street behind him, and he felt an intense heat brush against his back in a warm kiss. He didn't remember a sound, or even if he jumped or screamed or what. He turned around and saw a jeep smoldering in front of the offices, blood and guts and body parts from what looked like several people spread as far as thirty yards, and the old woman silently running away, her skinny legs shuffling back and forth. People lay around the wreckage, burned and dazed, and one was a uniformed young man, around John's age, and he was saying something to John and pointing urgently at the old woman, but he couldn't hear him. John ran to him and the man said, "It was her! Shoot her, man! Shoot her!"

John was no marksman, but he cocked his .45. Then there was a block of time he lost. Then he was standing over her, blood slowly collecting on the street around them, and he turned her over. Her bones were small like a bird's. The fact that he even hit her at all was unbelievable to him. The odds had to be enormous. The exit wound was within inches of her heart. She was breathing in and out deeply, her blood pressure steadily falling, staring up into the sky, past him, and then she looked into his eyes, and she smiled, the same smile she had given him when they passed in the street. Her purple scarf was lopsided, exposing gray hair. Her chest moved for much longer than he would have expected, maybe a minute or more. A bubble of blood formed around her lips, and she stopped smiling. With her last breath it popped.

6

The morning was always a rough time for John, but this was crazy. He lay on his back, staring at the ceiling. An arm and a skinny leg dangled off the side of the bed as if unable to convince the rest of his body to move. His head felt like it was lined with a thin metal sheet and someone was banging it over and over again with a ball peen hammer. Everything ached, from his toes to the muscles at the top of his neck. He wondered if his body had decided to shut down for good, and if he was in the process of dying. Nothing would surprise him at this point. He reached over to the top of the nightstand and felt blindly for his smokes. Relieved, he fingered the familiar package, flipped it open and pulled one out. Then he fumbled around until he found his disposable lighter. He lay in bed and smoked, ashing on the wood floor. He thought he might be embarrassed to be found if he died right now, smoking in bed, but ultimately decided that he didn't care. Maybe he would drop the smoke and burn his house down. But then his cats would die, and he didn't want that. He snubbed the cigarette out between his fingertips. Ash and stinky tobacco crumbled to the floor.

Slowly he started to roll over, growing even more alarmed at the sharp pains and stiffness that permeated his flesh. Christ, he was a zombie. He pushed himself up by the arm and raised his torso, crying out as he rose and then fell back into bed. He needed to ignore the pain and jump up like a jackrabbit. That was always the best course of action. Once he was moving, everything would fall into place. Blood would flow properly and things would work themselves out and stop hurting. That was how he usually got up. But it wasn't working now.

About half an hour later he made it into the bathroom, almost able to stand up straight. He stared at the broken old man in the mirror. His left eye was now totally black and blue where the cop had punched him. His other eye had a small cut above it and some kind of rash where Mello's watch must have scraped him. He needed a shave, and one of his teeth had poked almost all the way through his lower lip. His nose was crusty with blood, even though it was fine when he went to bed that night. He rubbed his upper lip, trying to scrape the flecks of blood away from his whiskers. His neck was bruised yellow all the way around from being choked.

He couldn't go job hunting like this. It would need to wait a day or two, at least. He had one more paycheck from Las Cruces Limo, which would cover his mortgage, and he had a little bit in the bank, maybe a grand. He often moaned to himself that he'd never learned a trade that paid a high salary, but never so often as when he was between jobs.

After the inventory of his wounds and some careful teeth brushing, he started the shower. The warm water felt good, but didn't have the magical effect he'd hoped for. When he was finished, he shaved and got dressed carefully, making sure his clothes were neat and pressed. He was of a mind that if you were down, getting everything together in normal order might jolt it all back into place. It certainly couldn't make it worse.

He fed the cats, and searched for something to eat for himself, but didn't find much in the cabinets or fridge. Typically in this situation, he might have strolled over to Laura's Diner for some pancakes and sausage, but that was out of the question, so he settled for black coffee and one end piece of toast, with butter.

He re-read Caroline's letter at his kitchen table as he sipped his coffee. It was nice of her to write him. He hadn't made himself easy to find. He didn't cry this time as he read slowly, deliberately, observing the curve of each handwritten word, the indentation from the pressure of the pen, looking back across all that time passed, like an ocean she had managed to cross to touch him. He could hardly believe it. It was like an old dream coming back to life. The internet was good for something, after all.

He looked over the part that mentioned his father's passing again. It made no mention of whether he had asked to see John in the last moments of his life. It made no mention of a desire for peace between them or feelings of remorse or guilt and though he had long ruled out ever talking to the old man again, now he found himself wanting to know. But as much as he wanted to write Carrie back, there was still a part of him that was frightened and not ready. He folded the letter and placed it carefully in its envelope as if it were a sacred text. Then he put the envelope in a cookbook on his counter.

He walked into the living room and decided he should clean the house. A few beer cans were leaned on top of the couch, against the window, and random pencils and assorted crap from an overturned cup on his desk were spread across the rug, courtesy of Merlin.

After picking up the debris and sweeping, he opened his front door and nearly tripped over Martin, who was curled up on his stoop. He had to grab onto the side of the porch and half hop over him, causing his whole body to tense up in pain. He cursed Martin and kicked at him, missing, and Martin wagged his tail happily and ran down the steps, looking back like he wanted to be chased.

"I'm gonna shoot you one day. Giddy asshole."

John drove to the bank and withdrew four hundred dollars, taking note that he only had six hundred and seventy-three left, after that. The papers were saying the economy was slowly but steadily improving, but there wasn't a sign of hope in Entierro. He gave serious consideration to dipping into the nearest bar so he wouldn't have to think about his impending doom for a few hours, but fought the urge and decided to go pay Aubrey back. Besides, he could always drink at home on the cheap.

The Next Wave Garage and Filling Station had an old rusted sign of a cartoon surfer riding a wave, which John thought was out of place in the arid environment they were in, but Aubrey was an interesting duck. He wasn't dumb like Mello, that was for sure, but he had his quirks. He had inherited the business from his father, after he died. His father had simply called it Gillis's. Aubrey renamed it after a self-described psychedelic surf band he and Carmello had been in at the University of New Mexico in the early eighties. Mello played bass and Aubrey played guitar, and the two still had jam sessions every so often in the garage space of the station, usually late at night, and Phil, the sheriff's deputy, was often called because of noise complaints. John would never admit to it, but he had called Phil himself on more than one occasion to complain about the horrible racket down the street.

When John pulled up to the garage, Old Jay Carruthers was seated out front in a lawn chair, sipping a Mountain Dew. He had on his usual faded red overalls, and when he noticed John, he simply raised his left hand without any expression, in greeting.

"What the hell happened to you?" he asked when he got a good look at John's face.

"Got in a fight."

"Well yeah. With who? Mike Tyson?"

"Is Aubrey here? I gotta see him quick."

"He's here." Jay motioned toward the garage door, which was around the corner of the building.

John found Aubrey underneath a car with only his legs exposed. He glanced around for Charlie Trout, and was relieved to not spot him. Charlie was Laura's son. He was a great mechanic. Aubrey had hired him three years ago, when Charlie was just twenty years old. The kid basically had no experience when he started, but he was a fast learner. Old Jay was supposedly a mechanic as well, but his arthritis kept him from doing much of that work anymore, so he mostly just sat out front, drinking Mountain Dew, and ran the cash register and chatted up pretty girls while he cleaned their windshields. He had been a friend of Aubrey's father, and had worked at the shop longer than anyone else. He was in his upper eighties.

"Got a minute?" John asked. Aubrey slid out from under the car, his face lined with black streaks and his forehead beaded with sweat. He blinked a few times, owlishly, behind his coke bottle glasses, and smiled when he saw it was John.

John had almost begun to speak when Aubrey said, "I heard."

"How? Mello?"

"I set his nose for him last night. Or pushed it mostly back into place. I'm not a doctor." Then he added, "He'll be fine. Sure is a screamer, though." He smiled so genuinely that John almost felt ill.

"Why didn't he go to the doctor?"

"He has a phobia about hospitals," Aubrey shrugged and reached for a filthy towel. "You know him. He's a different breed." He wiped his hands off, soaking up some of the grease, but spread most of it around. "So what's up?

Want to set up a card game this weekend? Give you and Mello a chance to patch things up."

"Look, I'm sorry…" he began, but Aubrey waved him away.

"You should tell him. I don't care. I'm sure he's earned a good beating or three over the years. But I will say that you're too old to be rolling around on the floor."

"I've got one or two left in me," John said. He reached into his pocket and pulled out two hundreds. "So I wanted to pay you back for getting my car out. I know I said I'd do it yesterday…"

"Wait 'till you get a job." Aubrey was shaking his head. "There's no rush. I ain't the bank."

"No, I can afford it. Here, take it." He shoved it into Aubrey's dirty hands.

"This is two hundred. It was only one-fifty."

"Just for the trouble, getting out the rig. I should give you more."

"C'mon, man, you know you don't have to worry about that."

John shook his head, and held his hand out as if he were telling a dog to stay. Aubrey folded the bills and put them in his front shirt pocket.

"Charlie not around today?"

"His day off. I bet Laura gave you an earful for starting a fight in her place. Boy, I would have loved to have heard that."

"Laura and I aren't seeing each other any more."

Aubrey took his glasses off and squinted at them before placing them back on his nose. "That's too bad. You only started dating a few months ago, but you really liked each other."

"I messed up, you know? I'm too old to mess up this bad."

"But it was just Mello. She'll forgive you, right? I mean I know it's not good for business, but...you had a moment of weakness."

"She made up her mind before that, apparently," John said, the words stinging him even as they left his lips.

Aubrey nodded and put his hands in his pockets. His arms had to bend around his belly to do it. Aubrey looked like something between a hobbit and a bear. "Charlie's gonna be bummed."

"What do you mean?"

"I think he thought you were good for his mom."

"That's awfully discouraging to hear now, Aubrey. Thanks."

"It's the truth. Besides, maybe she'll come around."

"I don't think so." John wasn't comfortable being this personal with people, even Aubrey, who he considered a friend. He didn't like appearing vulnerable. Besides, Laura wasn't coming around. She was going away. That was one thing age had taught him. He didn't entertain false hopes about women anymore. At least that's what he told himself. "I gotta go. I'll see you later."

John drove to Mello's house over on Pheasant St. without thinking. He sat in his van, parked across the street. He lit a cigarette. Some Merle Haggard played on the radio and a light mist fell from the sky, which had grown dark for one o'clock. The rain didn't wash anything away. It was only enough to make the world feel greasy. After the song was over John got out and walked to the front door. He knocked. There was some shuffling from inside, and then silence. John stood in front of the keyhole and then stared at his feet. He waited. The dead bolt clicked and the door creaked open. Mello appeared with a swollen red nose. He looked at John's face.

"Hey," he said.

"Hey."

"What's going on?"

"Nothing. Just in the neighborhood."

"Oh." Then, shortly, "You wanna come in?"

"Sure." John followed him.

"You want something to drink?" Mello asked, motioning towards the kitchen.

"Naw, I'm fine, thanks."

"I was just gonna smoke a bowl. You want some?"

John hesitated, and then said, "Sure." He looked around Mello's house. It wasn't so much dirty, as cluttered. A big poster of Al Pacino as Scarface was framed and hanging above the couch. Carmello sat cross-legged on the floor and motioned for John to sit on the couch.

"You see *Pineapple Express*?"

"What?"

"It's a movie."

"No."

"This strand is what they named it after. It's killer." Mello handed him a pipe stuffed with green buds. It was overflowing and looked sticky. John sniffed it. It smelled like a cross between bubblegum and pine needles.

"That like a *Cheech and Chong* movie?"

"Kind of, but not as good."

John decided to get his apology out of the way. If he waited much longer, Mello was likely to say something dumb that would make him not want to. "I'm sorry I broke your nose. I shouldn't have taken out my frustration on you. It wasn't your fault."

44

Mello looked down between his shoes. "I know. But I am sorry you got arrested. I was gonna tell you… before you hit me."

John nodded. "I'm a grouchy old bastard. I know it."

"Yeah you are." He motioned at the pipe in John's hand. "But let's put that behind us. Smoke."

John flicked his lighter and inhaled, igniting the buds in a crackling hiss. They curled and burned like an insect. He held in his hit for a moment, trying not to cough, and then exhaled the sweet smoke in a flurry that enveloped the entire area. He coughed slightly, his hand over his mouth. He handed the pipe to Mello.

"You ok?"

"Yup." John breathed in and out deeply, trying not to cough.

"It's good shit, isn't it?"

"Yup."

Mello took the lighter and inhaled the biggest hit he could possibly take, sputtering and spitting, trying to hold it in. Then he exhaled in an explosion, the whole room filling up with smoke, and they passed the pipe back and forth a couple of times in this fashion, until John was incredibly stoned.

"You know I respect you, man," Mello said, nodding seriously with narrow, bloodshot eyes. He pushed his hair back, away from his face, and grinned. His nose seemed even redder and bigger than it was before.

"Thanks," John said, not knowing what to say.

Mello spent the next half hour or so telling John about some movie he liked, called, *The Big Lebowski*. Or was it *The Big Chinaski*? Either way, he really wanted John to see it. He tried explaining the plot a few times and John wanted to follow it, but the more he heard, the more confused he became.

Mello perhaps sensed this, because he finally just said, "You gotta see it, man. You just have to see it."

When he finally left Mello's house they had each apologized about a dozen times. John was so high that he was a little worried about driving, which surprised him. The rain had stopped, and the sun was breaking through the clouds in sharp rays of light. He had to wear his sunglasses and even then he was squinting. He nearly took out a stop sign at the end of Mello's block, but then he leveled out. When he got home he did two shots of whiskey and took a nap.

He made himself an early dinner. When he was finished, he had a whiskey and a smoke on his porch while he watched the sun go down. A large cloud formation was stretched out along the skyline by a wind he couldn't feel. It got hung up on a ridge and its belly torn open, glowing the deep red of the evening magnificently.

After sunset he watched some television. There was a news story about negativity in the presidential campaign. He switched it to a *Leave it to Beaver* rerun. John loved *Leave it to Beaver*. It was an episode where the Beaver was caddying at a local country club. The man he was caddying for had made a bet with his friend, and Beaver had to keep score. The man was cheating by telling the Beave to write down strokes that were lower than he was actually hitting. He eventually won by just two or three strokes, and gave the Beave a five-dollar tip. At home that night, Ward mentioned that someone lost a five hundred dollar bet that day at the country club, to someone he never lost to before, and Beaver figured out it was the man he was caddying for. The next day he went to the man's office and reprimanded him for his deceit, and asked him how he would feel if his son, who was one of the Beave's classmates, were caught cheating. The man explained that he was sorry, but that he made the bet after "a few too many drinks" and he couldn't afford to loose five hundred dollars. Eventually they came up with a solution where the man bet his friend again, only this time the Beave cheated the other way, so the other man got his money back, and all ended well.

John turned off the TV and poured himself another drink before going back to his porch. Martin was curled up next to the brown wicker rocker. John lit a cigarette. He felt something like a calm. It was good, and he tried to hold onto it because he knew those moments didn't last. The moon was a thin luminous sliver, there was a healthy dusting of stars, and the night was cooler than usual. He drank half his glass of whiskey, eased into the chair and listened. Far off a coyote yelped. He saw Martin's ears perk slightly, but other than that, neither of them moved.

7

Over the next two weeks his depression slowly retreated like filthy water seeping back out of a flooded basement, exposing the dank and the rotten and the need for repair. He only called Laura once, but she didn't call back. He ate once at the diner when she wasn't around, and Piper was pleasant to him, but ultimately it made him feel strange to be there. He figured he needed more time. He wrote Caroline back and told her she and her new husband Gary should come visit him if they felt like it. He said he was sorry he wasn't with the family for the old man's passing, but that it was great to hear from his little sis, and he hoped she was happy.

Mello got him a job at Pearl's Hardware, which was where he worked part time when he wasn't supplying grass to local potheads. John was grateful for the work. He still hadn't heard from his public defender yet, but he wasn't really worried anymore. He felt like he could handle a few months in jail if he had to. He decided if that happened, he'd make Mello move into his house to take care of the cats and pay the bills. Mello wouldn't be able to say no. He took two really long hikes into the bush to relax, which helped clear his mind so he could come up with this new idea.

John woke in the middle of the night a few times, coughing. When he went back to sleep these episodes were usually accompanied by a nightmare. During one he dreamed that he was coughing up dead people, little three-inch bodies covered in mud and blood, fully clothed, slightly decomposed. He tried to catch them as they tumbled down his stomach so he could examine them, but they slipped through his fingers and disappeared.

Martin developed a curious habit of scratching on John's door late at night and then whining at him until he bent down to pet him, at which point he would bury his head in John's chest. He had never done anything like that before, but John began to develop some affection for the rascal, and welcomed his after-hours visits. He only tripped over him once, and he had lost the urge to kick him.

8

"Real men do love Jesus," John insisted, shaking his finger at Aubrey like a nun. Aubrey was being an incorrigible ball buster, which really pissed John off when they were playing poker. John privately felt a lot of confusion when it came to religion, but if he got drunk enough, he sometimes had a tendency to become strangely righteous and defensive of Jesus, though he didn't know why.

"Hey, my wife teaches Sunday school, so I can relate. I'm just making a comment about the broader social hypocrisy inherent in making a statement like that if you're an advocate of an unnecessary war. And I hate bumper stickers, particularly about religion or the Iraq war." Aubrey leaned back with a drunken smirk.

"I guess that's fair enough, but do you go to church?" John asked. He stopped shuffling the cards.

"No, I don't like it. You know that."

"Exactly!"

"But I believe in God, mostly. I just don't need to sit around with a bunch of self-righteous freakazoids to find him. I make my kids go."

"Mostly?"

"Mostly what?"

"You said you believe in God, mostly?"

"That's right."

"So how do you find him?"

"I listen to jazz."

"What the hell does that mean?"

Aubrey could hardly hide his delight. "I just don't know about all this absolutist dogma. You don't go to church either."

"I still love Jesus, I'm just angry at God."

"What are you even talking about?"

"I know what I'm talking about. I don't know what you're talking about."

"So shuffle the cards, and let's be content to be confused."

"Shit." John shuffled again.

Aubrey got up. "I'm gonna get another beer. You want one, Lowry?"

"Yes, you Godless heathen, I do."

Aubrey laughed out loud, his bellow roaring out of his chest like a warm fire. Mello, who was slumped back in his chair, almost asleep, perked up.

"I want one too," he said.

"Nope, you don't get one," Aubrey said, walking to John's fridge.

"Why not?"

"Because you're too drunk already. It wouldn't be fair."

"I'm going home, then."

"Fine, have another, you big baby. Just don't start whining when all your money's in other folks' pockets."

"I won't."

"That'll be the day." Aubrey opened the fridge, then called out to Charlie, "Trout? You?" Charlie nodded his mop of thick, curly, brown hair. Aubrey brought four beers back into the living room.

Old Jay was snoring, having become a notorious lightweight in his old age.

"Jay, it's your turn," John said. "Ante up!" He flicked a nickel at Jay's sternum.

Jay startled awake and clutched his chest. "What? What do you want?"

"It's your turn. Ante up or face further retribution, ya old coot."

"Now that was just foolish and unnecessary. What do you mean, scaring an old man like that? You're old enough to know better." Jay threw in his money and fell asleep before the round was even complete.

It was getting to be around one-thirty in the morning and John noticed that Charlie was yawning, and decided to chide him a bit. "Why are you tired? You're the young one here. You're supposed to be drinking us all under the table."

Charlie shook his head. "A bunch of lesbians came home late last night and woke me up. I had the windows open. They were outside my apartment yelling and falling down and puking and peeing in the bushes. It was like a frat party on the front lawn, but with lesbians."

"I'd venture to say that's unusual," Aubrey said.

"Too much testosterone. Just like guys. Did any of them start fighting?" John said.

"No. One of them started crying because her girlfriend broke up with her."

"A bunch of drunk lesbians on my lawn sounds like a dream come true," said Mello. "Did you see any of them making out?"

"A little. I was kind of tired. I'd already been up half the night," Charlie smiled. Mello nodded drunkenly and grinned back.

"Had yourself a lady friend, did you?" Aubrey asked, punching him in the arm.

"Anyone we know?" John asked.

Charlie clammed up and seemed to debate inwardly.

"Come on, tell us. We know who it is, don't we?" Mello yelled.

Charlie blushed. "It's Piper," he said.

"From your mom's restaurant? She's cute," Mello said, with buddy to buddy enthusiasm. "Good job, Charlie. And you don't even have to take her home to mom. She already knows her."

"You wanna hear a story about lesbians, I'll tell you one," John said, making a show of grabbing the attention of the table. He noticed Charlie was relieved to be out of the spotlight. "First of all, I should let it be known that all lesbians hate me. And this is why." He finished his beer and leaned forward, setting the bottle down on the table. "Back in about…oh, seventy-eight, I'd say, I was visiting an old high school buddy out in Hollywood. He thought he was going to be an actor, so he moved out there sometime while I was overseas. He was actually doing a lot of auditions that week, so I was hanging out at this coffee house and met a charming, beautiful young lady named Anna. We were having ourselves a swell chat, me and Anna, and I offered to buy her another cup of coffee. The guy behind the counter gave me a heads up and told me to be careful, because this girl's husband was just walking in the door. I turned around, and there was the biggest, baddest, bull-dyke I've ever seen. She was massive. She had sailor arms and linebacker shoulders. Truly, not someone to mess with. So I went back over and gave Anna her cup of coffee, and her husband and all her dyke friends were hangin' around, and I stayed and chatted with all of 'em. Well, this girl's husband knew something was up, and took a disliking to me, and gave me a hard time, and kind of started making fun of me. I persevered, and stuck it out like a gentleman, you know, did my song and dance, plus, I still thought I had a pretty good chance of getting in this hot little Anna's pants at some point, if I ever got her away from her hubby again. So they eventually had to leave, and I walked them outside, and low and behold, Anna's car wouldn't start. So I said, hey, pop the hood and let me take a look. Now looking at a car engine was and still is like staring at greek letters to me. I don't have a clue, but I was trying to impress this girl, so you know... Her husband starts to really rag on me, and starts saying what an idiot I am, and how I don't know jack shit about cars, and I don't know what happened, but I just snapped. I came out from under that hood and I punched her right in the face. Sent her crashing to the ground in a pile of massive limbs and denim. I figured I might as well finish it, because she must have outweighed me by about eighty pounds, so I jumped on her and started to pound away. All of her friends pulled me off of her, and she got up, and she pointed at me, and said, 'One day... I'm gonna see you on the boulevard. And when I do, you're toast, buddy.' So ever since then, all lesbians hate me. I think the word must have got out."

They all sat around the table in silence. Then Mello burst out laughing, and so did everyone else.

"You are so full of shit, man."

"Every word is true. You ladies believe what you want."

"I believe I'll get another beer," Mello said, shoving his chair out from the table and popping up. "Who else needs one?" Everyone grunted no, and he went to the kitchen. As soon as he was out of sight, they heard a loud shriek, followed by the sound of pots and pans crashing. Mello came tumbling into the living room with his hand on his neck and almost capsized the whole table. He took a huge breath and said, "It attacked me. The sonofabitch bit me."

"Who?" John asked.

"One of those damn cats, man." Charlie and Aubrey started to laugh. Old Jay looked confused.

"Merlin."

"He's the devil if you ask me. He was perched up there on top of the fridge waiting to pounce on me."

"I didn't see him in there," Aubrey said. "You sure you didn't just trip and fall into the counter?"

"The sadistic little bastard jumped on me like I was a piece of salmon. He actually bit me. Did he draw blood?" He bent down and pulled his hair away from his neck to show everyone.

"It's just a little red," Charlie said. "No blood."

"Are you sure?"

"Yes, he's sure. Stop whining, or I'll take you to the hospital," Aubrey quipped.

Mello sat down, rubbing his neck.

"Do you need me to go get you the beer?" John asked. "Did he frighten you that much?"

"I'm fine without. I can go back in a minute. Do you think he'll bite me again?"

"He might. He's probably just feeling ignored. I'll go." John lit a smoke as he got up and went into the kitchen. He mimicked Mello's scream as soon as he was out of sight.

"Nice touch, asshole." Mello said, but John started coughing and couldn't reply. He hacked and struggled for breath.

55

"You okay in there, buddy?" Aubrey said. John didn't stop, or say anything. He coughed harder. After a few seconds he was able to force himself to stand straight and open the fridge and grab the beer. Merlin was standing over in the corner amongst the pots and pans, watching him and purring. John left the kitchen and handed Mello his beer. He sat down.

"I'm okay. Merlin was licking his lips in there," he said.

"John, there's blood," Aubrey said.

John didn't get what he was saying at first. He thought he was talking about Mello being bitten. Then he saw they were all looking down at his arm. Blood was smeared across the forearm he'd coughed on. He felt wetness on his chin and wiped a dark red streak onto the back of his hand. If he'd been alone, he could have ignored it, but it was way too much blood to explain away in front of his friends. It seemed to be everywhere. How long had he been coughing? He tasted even more in his mouth.

They were all watching him, so he said, "Damn. I guess I need to go to the doctor."

9

"How long have you been a smoker, Mr. Lowry?" The doctor's eyes were all business, but his voice was distracted, thin and annoying. Maybe thinking about Maui. Or Puerto Vallarta.

"Since I was about fourteen." John looked at the x-ray hanging on the wall as if it held the answer. His lungs looked like they were each filled with about five or six cotton balls that had grown into each other. Little cloudy cobwebs.

"Well, it looks like we have a real problem."

"You can be blunt. I'm not one to bitch if I'm hung with a new rope."

"This is most certainly lung cancer. It's spread to both lungs, and although we still need to test to see if its spread beyond that, my guess would be that it's a strong possibility."

"And that's not good." John's head got so heavy he thought it might fall off and spiral to the floor. He turned his attention to a photograph of some pink and yellow flowers on the wall that looked like a greeting card. It didn't make him feel any better. He thought maybe they should have pictures that were proportionate to the heaviness of the topic being discussed. Like for what was happening now, maybe some tits would be nice. Maybe a little Ava Gardner, or a Jane Mansfield pin-up, for

Christ's sake. Hell, if someone opened a brothel across the hall they'd make a killing.

"No."

"So what am I looking at here?"

"Probably an aggressive regimen of chemo. Like I said, you'll have to have some more testing done, but it's probably stage four, judging from these x-rays. As you can see, it's…"

"How long would you guess?"

"I don't like to speculate about that. I find it's best to be positive and discuss those prospects candidly at a later date as you establish the best form or forms of treatment."

What was this guy, a robot? "Could you tell me what kind of time I'm looking at? Gimme the least and the most."

The doctor sighed and looked annoyed. "Could be as little as two or three months, or as long as a couple years, if you're lucky. Depends how you respond to treatment."

"Two or three months?"

"Maybe more. Maybe a lot more."

"But maybe less?" John felt like crying.

The doctor put his hand on John's shoulder, reassuringly, in his first real sign of humanity. "You need more testing before anything can be done, planned, or decided."

"But most don't survive? Stage-fours?"

"In the long run? No. But it's not unheard of. Listen, I would recommend not expecting a lot, but not losing hope, either. There're some wonderful success stories out there, even if the overall prospects are grim. But remaining positive is always seen as essential to putting up a good fight."

"Thanks for the advice."

John scheduled an appointment for the next week at the Albuquerque VA center. He didn't have health insurance, and the emergency room visit was going to be expensive. Aubrey had driven him and was waiting outside, reading a book. John felt bad for Aubrey because there was nothing really to say under the circumstances. At least nothing that would help. He was embarrassed for putting him in that position. He told him very simply what had happened and what had been said and lit a smoke and rolled the window down. Aubrey didn't say anything. He usually didn't care if John smoked in his truck as long as the kids weren't in it.

"Bad news always makes me want to smoke," John said.

"Me too. Gimme one of those."

"You don't smoke."

"About once or twice a year I do."

John was disappointed that Martin wasn't on his porch when he got home, but his cats both greeted him warmly. He did a shot of whiskey as soon as Aubrey pulled out of the driveway. Then he put away the card table from the night before, a cheap, fold out job. He cleaned up some bottles and vacuumed the floors.

When he breathed in heavily he felt pain in his chest. How long had that been happening? Months? Years? He hadn't really been paying attention. He just thought it was a normal, old man type of pain. He went to the bathroom and peed. How many times had he peed in his life? How many more times would he get to go before he died? How many farts? He tried to do the math, and gave up. He looked at his face in the mirror and splashed it with cold water. His eyebrows were like two craggy, forested ridges. The lines down his face, rocks splitting from the elements. His facial muscles sagged and drooped. Like the bad kids in gym class, they had no interest in participating.

John felt far away from everything and out of control, as if he were a small seed blowing across a vast, empty plain. He needed to rest. He sat down on the couch and felt something hard beneath him. He reached under the cushion and pulled out his gun. Staring at it, he felt the tug. For half a second he was almost there. Then he put it down next to his leg. He was too scared to do it. Even now, facing what he was. And yet there was no cosmic revelation. There was no deeper understanding or appreciation of life. It was the same as before except now he knew he was dying. He would wait for it.

10

"Check out my new propaganda," Mello said, motioning toward his television set.

"What is it?" John asked, closing Mello's front door behind him. He put his Tupperware container full of cookies on the coffee table.

"March to Honor. It's a new video game. You get to fight insurgents and the Taliban in Iraq. Check it out. It's crazy."

"Jesus. Is that legal?"

"Of course. It's a cool game, but damned if it isn't morally objectionable on some level, huh?"

"Who makes this stuff?"

"Probably the Pentagon, but I bet you'd be hard pressed to prove it."

John watched as Mello's American soldier, dressed in brown and tan army fatigues, broke down the door of an apartment building with the rest of his unit and proceeded to mow down brown skinned men in rags and turbans.

"Did you just cut that guy in half with your machine gun?"

Mello laughed. He seemed high. "Yeah. Crazy, right? Shit. You lose points for targeting civilians." One of his grenades had just blown up half a family running down the street.

"It certainly is something."

Mello dropped his controller and took a hit off his bong. "Oh, sorry," he said, putting the bong down and blowing his smoke away from John. "How's quitting going?"

"This nicotine gum doesn't work at all."

"So you're still smoking?"

"A little."

"When do you start chemotherapy?"

"On Friday. Do you want a cookie? Bonnie brought them by for me today."

"Sure. That was nice."

"Yeah, Aubrey did real well with that decision, didn't he?"

"Sure did. I wish she liked me more."

"What do you mean?"

Mello shrugged.

"No, really."

"She thinks I'm a bad influence."

"That's because she's smart. I've gotta go to work. I just thought I'd drop these off for you because I don't really go for sweets. But don't tell Bonnie or Aubrey I gave them to you."

"Alright. Have fun at work."

"Ok." John stopped at the door and turned around.

"Why is your nickname Mello Beans? Why not Spicy Beans, or something with a little flair?"

"Because my name's Car-mello Bencini."

"Yeah, I know. But is that ever gonna get you layed? I mean, keep you from spending all day kooked up in this dingy little house, getting high, and imagining that video games are being used as propaganda, even as you let them rot your brain away?"

"You think Spicy Beans is better? I'm not Mexican."

"Just brainstorming."

Mello threw a cookie and John heard it hit the door as he shut it behind him.

Pearl's Hardware was across the street from Laura's, and John parked behind it before heading into the diner to grab a coffee to go. As he was crossing the street, he saw Piper on the side of the building by the dumpster, talking to someone. She was a cutie, and good for Charlie, but John wished she didn't dye her hair strange colors. It took away from her natural look. The look that Laura used to have in spades, and still had plenty enough of.

He missed Laura. They hadn't dated long, but they sure had fun together. He flirted with her for months before deciding to risk catastrophic embarrassment by asking her out. After all these years, he thought it might have gotten easier. But it didn't, especially the breaking-up part. In fact, rediscovering the fun that could be had with a nice woman made it hurt twice as bad when it went away again.

As he walked up to the door of the diner, he turned and saw that Piper was arguing with a young man. She seemed to be telling him to get lost, and he wasn't listening. He looked really agitated. John waited, hoping that whatever was happening would dissolve quickly and peacefully, because he was in no shape to do anything. The kid was muscled, young, in his twenties. He had a very short haircut, military looking, and he wasn't a bad looking guy, except he looked like he wanted to knock Piper's head off her neck.

Luckily, they both glanced over and saw John standing there, and the embarrassment of being in public must have helped him calm down. But he wasn't happy.

John turned from them and opened the door slowly. He heard Piper say, "I don't want to have this discussion again."

The guy replied, "You're gonna have to. You can't just treat people like this and expect everything to be okay." John didn't hear anything else. He went inside and the couple parted ways, the guy to his Ford Explorer, which he gunned out of the parking lot in a hiss of gravel and exhaust, and Piper to the entrance at the back of the diner.

He didn't see Laura around, which was both disappointing and a relief. He hadn't even heard from her since his diagnosis. He figured for sure that Charlie must have told her and she would have made some effort to contact him. It hadn't been that long, though. Maybe he would hear from her soon.

Darla was behind the counter. He ordered his coffee.

As she poured it into the to-go cup he said, "You see that outside?"

Darla glanced around quickly and half whispered, "Ex-boyfriend. Just got back from Iraq. Won't leave her alone."

"What's his problem?"

"I don't know. She dumped him while he was over there, and now he's back. Guess he's pissed. He's kind of crazy, though. And not from the war, either. Just born that way."

"What did she say?"

"Well, actually, my brother Pete was in his battalion. I asked him about Bud because he's been bothering her, just to see if he was dangerous. He said that he was a good guy to have on your side, but that he's a rough customer. He wouldn't specify. He won't really talk about stuff that happens over there, but I got the impression that maybe not everything Bud did was legal. Pete clams up about it. I think Bud got discharged, but honorably. I told Piper what he said, but then she told me flat out that he joined the army to kill people. She said there wasn't anything to it other than that. And then she said she wadn't afraid of him and to forget about it, so…" Darla shrugged.

"Does she need to file a restraining order or something?"

"I don't know. Maybe. But don't talk to her about it or she'll get pissed. "

"What's his name again?"

"Bud. Bud White." Piper appeared from the back of the store, looking flustered, and Darla gave John his coffee. He paid for it and went to work.

He spent most of his evening shift framing a magazine cover for an ex-Playboy model. All the guys went nuts looking at it after she left. Good for her. She looked a little older now, but still not bad. Some hard living. The younger guys said they would have done her back then.

The cover shot was from nineteen sixty-eight. She used to be really something. It was a picture of her standing next to a saddle in a barn, which he figured she would be straddling a few pages in, and he was right, with nothing on but a cowboy hat. She had golden skin with a light dusting of little sexy freckles, and her supple breasts hung as if gravity existed solely to make them look that good. The lens the picture was shot with gave it a fuzzy glow. It must have been before airbrushing. She had bright pink nipples that stood at attention, probably from ice, but her flirty smile made it feel like it was you doing that to her. She had strawberry blonde hair, and a full bush of pubic hair. John liked the big bush. He didn't understand why every girl was shaving it these days. It was like an epidemic.

For his break he drove down to the Pump 'N' Run, a mile or so out of town. It was the only other gas station besides The Next Wave. He didn't want to see anyone he knew. He flipped through some magazines, and thought about the cancer that had already spread to his brain and his stomach. He found this out the week before. He couldn't catch a break. He hadn't told anyone the newest bad news.

As he skimmed the contents of one of the haughty New York magazines, he saw a picture of a frail, wrinkled old man the size of a baby. The anomalous dwarf was held up on display by an average-sized hand. John read the caption of the picture. It stated that it was actually a seven-week-old baby boy from west Darfur, suffering malnutrition and intestinal blockage. He looked back at the picture in amazement. His stomach dropped. Seven weeks old. The baby's hands had long, rough looking fingers, as if they had grown and been abused for years, deteriorating from arthritis and manual labor. His belly was distended and translucent, blue veins clearly visible beneath the dark skin, crinkled up like little rivers of sorrow. The flesh over the frail collarbone was sunken and stretched as over a rotting carcass in the sun. His face was an exercise in catatonic pain control, seeming to radiate a messianic aura, as if it were a classical painting of one of the great saints, or a starving monk, the eyes imbued with sadness and knowledge beyond all reckoning of man or beast.

John put the magazine back on the shelf and bought a package of Cool Ranch Doritos that he threw away after eating only three. His stomach ached. He went back to work before his break was over, and worked silently until they closed at eight. That night as he lay in bed, he prayed for the child and cried because he couldn't think of an idea to save him. Then he dreamed of a darkness that slowly consumed all things, and he welcomed it as it drowned out his mind's rabid flailing.

11

The second was a young man, maybe no older than seventeen, near a small village that sat on a river just west of the central highlands. Maybe nineteen sixty-six? The platoon was on a two-week hump through the bush, looking for enemy movement, and they hadn't seen anything.

Specifically, they were looking for a group of VC who had ambushed and cut another platoon by a third of its size. This had happened a week and a half ago, and then they had vanished into the jungle. They might turn up, or they might not. They had seen it all before. The firefight would come, or it wouldn't, and there was no real way to know. In the meantime, to break up the edgy boredom, Nash had something he was showing off to some of the guys- it was a necklace made of human tongues. There must have been forty of them, dark and shriveled, like dried chilies.

"Man, that's some fucked up shit. What are you, some sort of witch?" Darius Lyle asked, cringing.

"It's for protection," Nash said, his shirt unbuttoned. "Keeps the bad spirits away." He smiled like he was in a Wintergreen commercial.

Darius looked like he wanted to run away. Nash was a joker, but his sense of humor had become twisted over here, as had so many others. But they weren't his tongues.

At least he hadn't collected them himself. Nash wasn't that cold blooded.

Nash bought the tongues from a Green Beret who had collected them off the body of some other crazy Greenie after he died. John didn't know what he paid for them. Probably too much. He pictured Nash haggling the guy down as much as he could, just dying to wear them and freak everybody out. He pictured the hard-core Greenie holding out for a wad of cash because he didn't want to give away his dead buddy's war trophies. What was he going to do, send them to the guy's wife? He pictured Nash finally succumbing to an astronomical figure, just because he knew they would cause such a ruckus. That was just the sort of fucker he was.

He had woken John up early that morning to show them off. John was dreaming of a savage wasteland where men and animals, lions, wild boars, zebras, everything, were all eating each other alive in a massive bloody orgy, screaming and wailing into a crescendo of noise that finally sounded off like a thousand frenzied trumpets, so he was relieved to be awakened, but then very put off by the trophy around Nash's neck. Nash grinned and held his shirt open so John could see.

"What's that?" They looked like they stank, though he detected no odor.

"Tongues," Nash said, proudly. "Think they'll scare some of the guys?"

"What kind of tongues?"

"People's."

"Jesus Christ, Nash, no wonder my dreams are so fucked up." He slid back down into his foxhole to fetch some smokes.

"Yeah, but I bet this'll freak out Darius. Right?"

"Sure. Hell, he might faint and bump his head and get medevacked out of here. You'd be doing him a favor."

Later that afternoon, some of the guys were laughing at Nash's necklace as they descended into a small gully to investigate a village, which consisted of just a few scattered huts. Nash got up real close to Darius and asked if he wanted to maybe trade something for his trophy, since it was such a good luck charm and all, and at exactly the moment Darius Lyle turned away from Nash in disgust, three or four bullets hit him with a dull flapping noise, striking his breastbone. Two of the next shots hit Nash, one somewhere in the body, and the other in his head. Nash's blood and some of his brains sprayed across John's forehead and ran into his right eye.

John dropped down, half behind Nash, who had collapsed, and raised his rifle. Darius lay in front of them. A large blowhole in his chest sprayed a mist of blood with each rapid breath. About thirty yards beyond, John saw three boys shooting AK-47s into the squad from a small footpath connected to the main trail. As he aimed, other soldiers struck two down immediately. The third and smallest fell right after John started firing, and though he couldn't see very well, he was pretty sure he hit him at least once or twice, so he counted that one. Afterward, someone threw a grenade in a rage, and then there was nothing left but the smoke, blood, and twisted, broken bodies. It was over within six or seven seconds.

They ultimately reasoned that the VC were just a small patrol, maybe new recruits, not even really soldiers yet, who were caught off guard and panicked.

Darius died in minutes. Nash was dead before he hit the ground. John sat in the dirt for some time afterward, looking at the tongues around his bloody neck. Nobody touched them. At some point, he washed Nash's brains out of his hair in the river. It was the oddest sensation. Before the white zipper on the body bag was closed, John walked over to him and knelt down. In place of Nash's left eye was a dark, gaping red hole. His blonde stubble was now softly misted crimson. John cut the necklace off with his knife and tossed it in the river. He couldn't really explain then, but he didn't want anyone to see it but his friends.

As he watched the trophy disappear under the peaceful surface of the river, Ben Foster, a good ol' boy from west Texas remarked, "I guess it don't keep the bad spirits away after all."

12

John didn't go to Chemotherapy. He sat outside the VA hospital, in his van. Then he left and bought a carton of cigarettes.

It wasn't that hard of a decision. He just didn't want to go in there. As he smoked and drove himself home, he cried and wondered what his sister would say when he finally told her he was on his way out. He wanted to come up with some way of making it not sound so bad. That wasn't going to be easy.

The next day the ex-Playboy model came back into Pearl's to pick up her framed cover, and they started talking. She was giving him the right signals, so he figured, what the hell? They went back to his place and had a couple of whiskeys. They talked about pets and movies and then had sex and then talked for a while more. It was nice. She lay across him, her breasts real and surprisingly still ok to look at and touch. Her name was Claire. She kissed him on the cheek and they laughed, and she told him about her days as a model. He asked her if she ever slept with anyone famous. She said she had sex with Frank Sinatra once. After he heard that, John got excited and they tried to do it again, but he couldn't finish, so they went to sleep. She didn't seem to mind.

In the morning he woke to someone knocking at the front door. He coughed and staggered slowly out of bed.

His mouth was stale. Claire lay half covered in the sheets. He put on a shirt and pants and opened the door.

It was Laura. She was in her work uniform, her hands folded in front of her apron. She had been crying. Mascara was still smeared across her cheeks.

"Laura?" He panicked for a moment. She would want to come in. Claire was in his bed.

"I was trying to call you. You're phone's off the hook."

"Oh." He looked back and saw the phone lying on the floor next to the couch. One of the cats must have knocked it off its base the night before. "Are you alright?"

"Piper's dead."

The words flew through his brain too fast and didn't stick. "What?"

"Charlie found her in her apartment this morning...she didn't show up to work yesterday." Laura crumpled and sat down on the steps. She cried out and put her face in her hands.

"How? Are you sure?"

Her head shook back and forth violently. "Charlie's devastated," she said between sobs. "My poor baby. John, I don't know what to do with him. He said they were in love. I didn't even know they were dating."

John knelt down and put a hand on her shoulder. He felt like he was dreaming, like he might wake up any moment.

"I didn't even know," she cried. "How could I not know?"

13

Charlie had found Piper tied to her bedposts, naked and gagged, her throat cut and her face so battered that part of her jawbone was protruding. They couldn't have a funeral for over two weeks, so the county could perform an autopsy. When it finally came, skin from under her fingernails and the semen in her torn vagina matched the DNA samples from hair they'd taken from Bud White's apartment, but they couldn't find him anywhere. He had friends who had last seen him recently, but they weren't sure exactly when. He was just gone, as if he'd never come home.

Piper's parents both died when she was young, and she had no other family, but some of the town turned out for her funeral. Her murder hit everyone hard, but Mello cried for three days straight. Charlie was catatonic throughout it all. Laura was strong for him. She didn't cry much at the funeral, but she stroked his back and neck, and held him as he stared solemnly at the ground, his face pale and gaunt from not eating.

John heard all sorts of strange rumblings about Bud, whispers between old ladies at the diner, and more elaborate denunciations from men at Pearl's counter. He figured maybe less than half of it was true, but who really knew? If you believed the rumors, Bud White was pure evil, and had been terrorizing the countryside with his nefarious deeds almost since birth. When he was only seven, the sheriff two counties over, in San Miguel, called his father because he caught him sniffing girls' bicycle seats. His mother died when he was a baby. He picked on children who were smaller and weaker than him at school, taking particular delight in torturing the handicapped or blind students. He stole his first car at fifteen. He was arrested for assaulting the referee of his high school wrestling match at sixteen- he head-butted him for disqualifying him, giving the man a concussion and headaches for the rest of his life. He was also was arrested for public intoxication countless times, minor drug dealing, and eventually shaped up enough to join the army after 9/11.

The rumors circling his departure from the service were worse. Depending on whom you talked to, he had raped and killed several young Iraqi women before it all got too big to ignore, and they gave him an honorable discharge, or he had a hand in the massacre of a family who was trying to flee a combat zone and stabbed a sergeant who was trying to have him held accountable, or several combinations thereof.

A year before he shipped out for Iraq, he apparently met Piper somehow, and they began some sort of relationship, although John couldn't imagine what she could have seen in him, being as sweet as she was, and especially taking into account that she went on to date Charlie, who was about as nice and sensitive a young man as one was likely to find.

The only thing he was certain of was that Bud White was the first person in his entire life that he had a deep, personal desire to kill.

14

In the wake of it all, Laura and John rekindled their friendship, although there was to be no romance. She couldn't ever have another romance. She had sworn it off for good and she told him so. But she hugged him hard and she told him she would always love him. She also gave him a look like she was going to carve his liver and told him if he didn't go to chemo so he could live a little longer and reconnect with his sister, she was going to make him sorry. He started on a regimen the next week.

Charlie stopped going to work. Aubrey let him take an indefinite leave of absence. He moved out of his apartment and started staying with Laura, just until he got back on his feet. He spent his days either sleeping at her house, or drinking his meager savings away at bars. One afternoon she convinced him to trim a tree in the yard for her, just to get him out doing something physical, but he slipped and cut his left thumb nearly clean off. Most of the time he sat on the couch with his hand balled up in a big white bandage and cried, switching the television between *Wheel Of Fortune* and *Mythbusters*.

He lost weight and stopped shaving. Laura tried to get him to go see a therapist, she even offered to pay for it, but he just looked at her with those big, brown, sad eyes, and she left him alone.

It hurt her to see him like this. She didn't want him to have a broken heart. She wished she could take it away and keep it all inside herself where it couldn't hurt him anymore. Years ago his father, Cleaton, had nearly broken him as a child. That was why she left. But this was something she couldn't protect him from.

If she just kept feeding him and letting him rest, he would get better. She would just keep feeding him. It would work, she told herself.

Taking care of Charlie took so much out of her that she almost didn't have the energy to be at the diner. There certainly wasn't any time for her to grieve on her own. Darla became the de-facto manager for a while. She hired some new girl named Stacy to take Piper's spot. Nobody liked her.

No one played Piper's favorite songs on the jukebox- No *La Isla Bonita*, no *Sgt. Pepper's*. If something that she used to play a lot did come on, the staff would become noticeably agitated. It did not pass quickly.

"You know why," John said one night when she brought him dinner. He had been to chemo that day, but he wasn't too sick from it. "Because she was charmed. She was like a movie star in real life, every day, for everyone to be a part of. People like that. It makes them feel special too."

They sat in his living room, eating a grilled chicken salad with walnut dressing that she'd thrown together. She was impressed with him tonight. She rarely heard him speak so much. He was usually more reserved and ashamed of his smarts. His face looked innocent right now. He had lettuce on his chin. She reached across him and wiped it off. He smiled shyly.

"Don't eat too much. You don't wanna get sick," she said. He had lost a little weight, maybe five pounds or so. He looked tired, but was cheerful.

"You know it doesn't make sense, her going before me." He put his plate down and let Merlin lick the leftover dressing. "Why doesn't God just take the ones who're eligible, like me?"

"I stopped wondering about what made sense to God a long time ago." They stared at Merlin as he licked the plate. After he was finished she picked up the dishes and dumped them in the sink. "Can you clean up by yourself?" she asked. "I want to get back home to Charlie."

"Sure. Still not doing well?"

"No." She came out of the kitchen and wrapped her hands around each other. "Don't you go and smoke as soon as I leave."

"I won't," he said, and stood up to walk her out. She knew he would smoke. And she was pretty sure he knew she knew.

When she got home, Charlie was on the couch, watching television. He said hello. She greeted him and went to bed. She turned her floor fan on high to muffle the sound of her sobbing and lay in the darkness, her face buried in her pillow. She cried for a long time and later, after she stopped, a couple of cars buzzed by in the dense quiet. She couldn't help herself from picturing Bud White behind the wheel of one of them, roaming the world freely, and she imagined herself stalking and killing him over and over again, each time in a different way. In the morning's early hours, she finally calmed down and drifted into a dreamless sleep.

She woke at about nine a.m., put on her bathrobe and washed her face. Charlie was still on the couch, sleeping. She pulled a knit blanket up to his chin and watched his chest rise and slowly fall. When he began to stir, she went into the kitchen and started a pot of coffee and some eggs.

15

The day was a clear mid-June roaster, a little dry, a little more hot. John was bent over on the side of the road next to his van. His legs were set far apart, to keep from splattering vomit on his shoes. He was already late for work, so he was worried about his shoes. His chest burned and he was sweating. After vomiting, he wiped his mouth on a handkerchief and took four generic aspirin from the middle console of the van. He drank them down with some coffee from a thermos, rinsed his mouth out, gargled, and spat.

He rolled up the window to keep the cool air in the van and stepped on the gas. The vehicle lurched forward unsteadily, like a hunchback.

He got to work twenty minutes late, but felt slightly better. As he opened the small locker where his crisp blue work-apron was kept, he heard two of the guys talking around the corner, near one of the sinks. It sounded like Luke and Casper.

"Civil War veteran is late again." Luke laughed.

"He must have left his saber at Gettysburg," Casper said. "Too bad, since it takes him all day to get anything done. I swear, when are they going to fire that guy? He's absolutely worthless."

"I'm tired of covering for his ass. He's late almost every day, and when he isn't, he's calling in sick."

"I'm all for keeping the elderly employed, you know, giving them something to do, but you've gotta draw the line somewhere."

"In the sand."

"What?"

"I said you draw a line in the fucking sand, dude."

"Oh, yeah." And with that they both started laughing at a joke that John didn't get. They sounded like a couple of queens. Did they really think that about him? That he was a worthless, slow, old person that needed to be put to pasture?

He considered rounding the corner and confronting them, the little cocksuckers. He wanted to tell them that he was sick, and to watch the mouthy bullshit, or he'd knock their teeth out the back of their ignorant little brains.

He wanted to tell Casper that on a good day he looked like a Puerto Rican whore, with his eyeliner, dark lipstick, and dumb-ass chains around his neck. Instead, John rolled his apron up and put it back in his locker. Closing it softly, he held his keys tight, so as not to make a sound, and walked back out the door into the bright sunlight.

When he got home, he called Mello.

"Will you take care of my cats for a few days?" he asked, pulling his old sleeping bag down from the top of his closet.

"What for?" Mello was chewing on some sort of crunchy food.

"Going on a trip."

"Where to?"

"Camping. Don't talk with your mouth full."

"You called me, man." He then crunched especially loud, and drew it out for a long time, smacking his lips. Then John thought he heard him say, "I don' know man, I'm scared of the one…Gandalf."

"Merlin."

"Huh?"

"His goddamned name is Merlin." John said, just wishing Mello would shut the hell up and say yes.

"Okay, Christ, calm down. He bit me that time, remember?"

"I'll leave a squirt bottle by the front door. Just use that if he bothers you."

"Will it work?"

"Of course it will work. I do it all the time." John was lying.

"Because he's a mean son of a bitch, John."

John sighed. "I know. But I said it'll work. It's like his kryptonite."

"Alright, I'll do it. How long you gonna be gone?"

"About a week. Maybe a little more. There's plenty of food for them. I'll call you when I get back." He thought of something else. "Hey."

"Yeah?"

"The key will be under the mat."

"I was gonna ask, but I forgot. Wait, what about your shifts at work?"

"Luke and Casper are covering for me."

An hour later, John packed a backpack, and tied his sleeping bag to the top in a roll. He put it in the back of his van, along with a small lantern, a bottle of whiskey, and a portable Coleman stove. The stove was missing a knob on the left burner, but he had a pair of pliers in the toolbox under his front passenger seat. He threw some extra blankets in as well, and slid his pistol snugly between the folds. A box of ammunition was crammed between a spare tire and the wall.

He fed the cats. Mello would come by in the morning. Afterwards, wandering the yard and smoking a cigarette, he realized he was waiting around for Martin, but the mongrel was nowhere. As he ground his smoke into the sandy dirt, a scorpion scurried by. He dug in his heal to snuff out that small life and decided it was time to go. It was cooling off a little. The sun had withdrawn behind some bluffs to the west, causing the entire skyline to glow a deep orange, as if there was a vast bowl of Jell-O hovering in the stratosphere, preparing to crash to earth.

16

John arbitrarily chose to travel south on two eighty-five for four and a half hours and pulled his van into the parking lot of a motel about forty miles north of Roswell. He cleared some space in the back and rolled his sleeping bag out. He had forgotten his watch and didn't have a cell phone, but figured it was after two a.m. The night air was clear and a high crescent moon cast a soft glow over the hills.

After a few peanut butter crackers and some pulls off the whiskey, he lay down and smoked a cigarette. He stifled his cough and put out the butt in the rim of his spare tire, until he could throw it out in the morning.

Still unable to fall asleep, he found an old deck of cards in the glove box and played solitaire by the glow of a small flashlight on his keychain. About half an hour later it ran out of batteries, so he snuck over to the ice machine and stole a plastic cup so he could pour a big nightcap on the rocks.

He woke up sometime late in the morning and nipped the bottle again to make his small hangover disappear. There was movement outside the van, probably people checking out and getting back on the road. He peeked out the window and saw a young boy staring at him from a toddler's car seat. The child held a donut and his face was smeared with chocolate. He didn't smile at what must have looked to him like some strange creature.

John rolled over and laid down again until he heard the family drive away. Then he peeked again, saw no one, and crawled into the driver's seat. Pushing in the car lighter, he fished a smoke from the crumpled box in the middle console, and backed out of the parking space. After a moment he had to pull over to cough. He threw his bloody handkerchief on the passenger floorboard.

At around two in the afternoon he felt up for breakfast, so he grabbed a pre-made ham and egg sandwich from a small gas station and a coffee. He'd been heading west for some time now, and could see the Rockies rising out of the earth like soft, penciled sketches. For some reason they weren't beautiful to him. Only cold, enormous and ancient.

After eating, he washed himself in the restroom, brushed his teeth and shaved. The mirror was a scratched up piece of metal screwed into the wall. Even taking that into account, the reflection of his flesh was pale and sickly. Passing the front counter on his way out, he glanced down at a newspaper. He stopped. On the right side just above the fold it read: WOMAN KILLS NEWBORN WITH SAMURAI SWORD. HUSBAND SAYS SHE WAS DEPRESSED AND HOPES SHE BURNS IN HELL.

17

Somewhere near the Arizona border he stopped at a roadside bar. It was off the main highway, dingy and old. It stank of urine, sawdust, and stale beer rings on tables. The bartender was a bored looking woman with a flashy hairdo that only succeeded in making her look sadder. There were a few people scattered throughout the dimly lit building. Pool balls periodically cracked just loud enough to eclipse any conversation, somehow making the place feel emptier than it was. No music came from the jukebox. It was like the purgatorial waiting room to a substandard afterlife.

John ordered a whiskey and sipped it. The other patrons paid him no mind, so he sat and watched. A young couple played pool. They were attractive. It looked like the guy was teaching her how to hold a cue without stabbing somebody. She giggled as he pulled her closer to him and whispered something in her ear.

John would have traded places with either of them in a second if he could. But he couldn't, so he decided to have another whiskey.

When the bartender came back around, he motioned to his empty glass.

As she poured, he produced a folded newspaper clipping of Bud White from his back pocket. He opened it gingerly and faced it toward her. "You seen this guy around here?"

She looked at John. His heart was banging in his ears. Then she looked at the picture. "Good looking kid. Can't say I have." She looked back at John. "You a cop?"

"No. I'm working for the family of a girl he's accused of murdering."

"Oh my. Like a private eye?"

"Something like that." He was going to die in jail. He was just sure of it.

"Sad story. Must be hard, the work you do." She began to turn.

"You sure you haven't seen him?" John called out to her a little desperately. "Supposedly he has family in Arizona. He may have come through here a few weeks ago."

She looked again, squinting at the crumpled photo. John handed it to her and she took it into better light, over by the cash register. "He does look a little familiar, I guess. I'm sorry, but I can't tell for sure. We get a fair number of strangers in here."

After paying for his drinks, John drove to the nearest hotel parking lot he could find to start getting ready for bed.

18

For the next three days he drove back and forth along the Arizona border, searching bars, strip clubs, gas stations, even a small church at one point, for any sign of Bud, but there was nothing. He got a number of strange looks, although none that led him to believe anyone would call the police about him. But he was feeling worse by the day and couldn't keep this up.

On the third day he picked up two hitchhikers, a homeless couple. He only picked them up because the girl seemed so young that it worried him, but when he saw her closer she looked to be about twenty. Although vagrants, they were perfectly healthy, aside from their dress and hygiene. Her name was Panera, and the guy was Blossom. She said they were rainbow people. From what John could tell, they were just hippies with a new name.

Panera's skirt was made from a patchwork of different flags, fabrics, and what appeared to be slices from a parachute. She had no modesty. She wore no bra. Her hair was a tangled mess, her underarms unshaven, and John could see an entire tiny breast when her loose, army-green tank top hung just so. He was both embarrassed and a little turned on at the sight.

"We're jugglers." Panera said proudly. "What do you do?"

"No kidding. What do you juggle?"

"Whatever, balls, bottles, hammers, flaming torches." Panera began to talk, and nobody else said anything for the next thirty minutes. John had never heard anything like it. She just talked, and talked, like a little cartoon chipmunk on speed. She talked about her home life before she ran away when she was sixteen, some old boyfriend named Sully or Sally, her favorite animal, polar bears, her favorite movie, *Point Break*, and so much more that John failed to catch as his concentration began to waiver amid a bout of exhaustion and pain.

What he gathered from her hectic speech was that between camping trips with other hippies, where they partied, took drugs, and then juggled various objects that had the capacity to inflict serious damage if they landed on one's head, Blossom and Panera liked to hitchhike or hop trains.

"Why do you travel that way?"

"It's fun."

"You meet a lot of interesting people," Blossom said sleepily, then let out a soft belch and lay down out of sight. A light snore rose from behind Panera.

"He's so cute," she said. "He saved me you know." Her eyes had a nice sparkle. She leaned out onto the middle console, watching the road ahead.

"What from?"

"A life of servitude. Of cold, corporate domination." She crawled over the console into the front passenger seat. Once situated, she rolled down the window and hung her leg out. Her shins were covered with wispy blonde hair, and her underwear, in full view for a moment, had Scooby Doo on them.

John didn't know what to say, so he said, "I guess you must be lucky."

"Yeah, I guess I am. I never really thought about it like that. Like, so…Big Picture…like you can't see the forest for the trees. Right on."

Confused, John focused on the road, on the shrubs and rocks passing in brown and green streaks on either side of his vision.

After a few minutes, Panera asked, "Are you ok? You look kinda tired."

"I am tired."

"You want to take a nap in the back?" She looked behind her. "There's still plenty a room next to Blossom. I don't have a license, but I know how to drive."

"That's ok. I'll be fine."

"Ok. Sure."

"I'm dying."

"Really?"

"Yes."

"What from?"

"Cancer." John pulled a smoke from the pack in his cup holder. He lit it and grunted, stifling a small cough.

"Mind if I bum one of those?"

"This is what I'm dying from. You want to look like this someday?"

She smiled. "I don't smoke that much. I won't do it when I'm older." She grabbed one from the pack, and clicked the lighter.

"Pretty soon I'll be so sick I won't even be able to wipe my own ass."

"Some joke, huh?" She inhaled and blue smoke left her pale pink lips and flew out the window.

"Yeah." John cracked his window to get a cross breeze going.

"I'm sorry you're dying. I didn't say that just a second ago, but I meant to."

"It's ok. I'm sorry I let you have that cigarette."

"You couldn't have stopped me. Well, since you bummed it to me, I guess you could, but you know what I mean. Don't get all guilty on me."

"I won't. Saying you're sorry won't keep me from dying either, but it was a nice thing to say."

"Are you scared?"

"Yes."

"But there's nothing you can do about it."

"Nope."

"Is it imminent?"

"Yes."

Panera nodded seriously, probably in the same way she had seen others do when speaking of death. "I suppose that's where we all end up, though."

"I'd rather not die so painfully, if you want to know the truth. But yeah."

"It hurts a lot?"

"My entire body feels like it's alternately burning and rotting from the inside. The chemo wasn't working, so I stopped."

"You're just stopping?"

"The cure's worse than the illness."

"So what are you doing out here in the desert?"

John breathed in deeply through his nose. "Just taking a little vacation."

"Like crossing it off the list?"

"What list?"

"The list of things you want to do before you die: Drive through the desert with a brilliant, charming woman."

"Guess I can check that off."

19

The late afternoon sun pierced John's eyelids, causing him to stir. He opened them to the glare. First a ball of white light and then colors, shapes. An awful stench. He was lying on a blanket in the grass. He wondered why. His thoughts were becoming ever more elusive and difficult to catch, but they were still in there. They had a picnic, he and the hitchhikers. Blossom and Banana. No, Panera. He rolled over and got up. The blanket was covered in puke right next to where he had been laying. It was also on his shirt.

He was at a rest stop, in a little patch of dry grass away from the benches and barbecue pits. It was coming back to him. They'd gotten some food at a gas station about thirty miles back, the canned corn which was now half digested and crusted onto the front of his shirt, and some sandwiches and fruit that looked like they could have been mixed in too. He couldn't remember how much he'd eaten. He'd put it all on his only credit card, which had a thousand dollar limit, was his only remaining source of funds, and was almost maxed out.

But where were the kids? John eyed the rest stop. There were two families, a truck parked, no van, and no dirty kids. He felt his back pocket. His wallet was gone. His mind reeled at the reality of the situation as he stumbled to the bathrooms to check for them, and then came out and looked again. He went back into the bathroom and washed his face, cupping his hands together to drink from the rusty faucet. The water was stale and tasted like iron, or blood. He took off his shirt and rinsed it in the sink, wrung it out as best he could, and put it back on. At least it was warm outside, and he would dry fast. But he felt cold from the inside.

He sat in the sun and didn't feel better. How could he let this happen? He'd only been down for a second. Ten years ago this never would have happened. He would have been smarter. No wonder that small-tittied tart had been so smiley and nice. No wonder she had made such a point to show off her ass, bending over, crawling into the back of the van, looking for the picnic blanket. Is it this one here, John? She'd looked back, wide-eyed and pouty-faced, the cartooned underwear riding up her ass. Is it this one? They were grifters. Goddamned hippies. How he'd fallen. Did he really think he had a chance? A battered, ugly old dog like him? Did he really think that she was going to take him into the bathroom, or out behind the bushes to fuck him, perhaps while Blossom slept? Give him one last rough ride on the poon-tang trail? Maybe he had. What an old fool.

The lighter was still in his back pocket. Looking on the ground for a brief moment yielded a half-smoked menthol. He lit it gratefully, inhaling the musty, mint flavored tobacco. He coughed. Then he puffed again and wheezed, his throat feeling like it was closing. Another drag before throwing the smoke to the ground. He couldn't breathe right. His chest and back muscles tightened, trying to force oxygen through his restricted airways. It was getting harder and harder to pull air in. Blowing it out was easier, but pulling it in felt like breathing through a very small straw, the kind for stirring coffee.

The two families had left. He was alone and it was getting bad. He leaned over a bench and tried to cough. Was he going to die now? He began to panic. He wasn't ready. He wanted to see his sister, wanted to meet her children. He started to pray frantically. He prayed for just a little more time. He couldn't die alone at some rest stop in Arizona.

"Oh God, God, God," he moaned between frenzied gasps for air. Just let him kill Bud White. Give him the time, give him the strength, give him the will. Let him take life again. Please give him purpose. Please give him more life. He demanded it, begged and cried a horrid moan from inside his gut, saliva sputtering between his gritted teeth and down his chin. He knew he didn't deserve it, but he fought anyway, cursing God for not letting it come easier.

He hated himself, and he hated every moment of his miserable, pathetic existence. He focused his hatred and disgust into his labored breathing, into a little ball of white-hot fire in his chest, and he told himself if he could continue to imagine this fire, he could stay conscious. He did this even as it got harder to keep going, as less and less life flowed through his swollen, ruined capillaries.

"Please, please, please, please…" he thinly wheezed. "I'm scared."

He collapsed to his knees on the blanket in the grass and leaned forward, stiffening and straightening his back a little to get the maximum amount of air. Needles of pain shot through the sore, weak muscles in his back and chest.

Close to an hour passed like this, and eventually he could tell it was going to get better. Another hour passed agonizingly, each shallow inhale promising just slightly more purchase than the one before. But he didn't get better enough to move.

Night was coming soon. A trillion sunbeams squirmed on the horizon like an army of golden ants devouring a carcass. As the day grew a little cooler and darker he continued his master study of the stitch and pattern on the blanket because that happened to be the easiest thing to look at. A very long time passed before he noticed a can of chicken soup sticking out from under a fold at the corner. It must have been leftover from lunch. He crawled to it slowly, careful not to exert himself too much. It seemed to take forever. When he overturned the edge of the blanket there was a bottle of water hidden as well. He opened it and drank as much as he could. After several tries, he was able to get his finger under the pull-tab on the soup. Still leaning over, he grabbed ravenously at the meat and vegetables as best he could with his fingers, chewing bit by bit, and resting when he had too. When he'd gotten all he could with his hand, he drank a little of the tepid broth and tossed the container in the general direction of a trashcan. It sloshed against a rock. He wiped his hand on a pant leg.

A little cold, John rolled himself up in the blanket once he could breathe easier and thought of Laura. He wished he were in her kitchen, enjoying a meal and her company. Just to smell her, feel her, and talk to her. He wished he hadn't messed all that up.

He saw Laura as his last chance for a normal life. He had felt for a very long time that he'd missed his chance, but he wasn't sure at what exact point it slipped through his grasp. It seemed as though it must be there somewhere, at some turn, some action taken, or opportunity lost, and he was always looking for a door that would put him back on course, but that was just what was so frustrating. Since he'd never known where he went wrong, maybe he was screwed from the start. He was starting to feel like it wasn't one or two things that threw him off course, but a lifetime of choices that were all moving toward one way of being, which was the way he was and he simply didn't have the ability to take his life where normal people went. Perhaps it lay dormant in his DNA, like power surging through a wall with no outlets.

But he supposed it didn't matter much anymore, since he was all out of chances.

So he sat in the rapidly cooling, but still warm night, wrapped in the picnic blanket like a refugee and wondered where this void came from, wondered for the thousandth time, as if there would finally be an answer, like some twisted monk trying to levitate a rock, always quiet, never moving, never stopping because he knew they were the same pointless matter. For some that was a reason to persevere, for others a reason to give up. But a rock holds no blood.

As he lay on his side and began shivering with fever, sweating through his clothes, he fought hard to concentrate on breathing and briefly worried about scorpions or a rattlesnake crawling in his bed, but then wondered why he should care so much about getting stung or bitten and then finally sleep graced him like an ill-fitting coat.

20

He woke with the first light, emerging from his cocoon like some ugly desert hatchling, doomed to live only one day, and filled his water bottle in the restroom. He was still feverish, but felt a little better. He coughed red. His stubble was long and all white. He looked homeless.

The rest stop had some visitors in the early grey morning, but his pride wouldn't allow him to ask for help. Sticking his thumb out at passing cars was one thing, but walking up and intruding on someone's picnic or catching them on the way to the bathroom was quite another. After stuffing the bottle of water in his back pocket, he folded the blanket and put it under his arm. Then he saw some string tied to one of the picnic tables and walked over to inspect it. Probably some folks tying their darn kid to the table, he thought. The string was in good shape and there was a lot of it. He looked over his shoulder and bit it off and wrapped it around either end of the rolled up blanket, then bit off four smaller pieces and doubled those into pairs to make straps so he could wear it like a backpack. Finished tying his bed together, and headed east, toward home, he stuck out his thumb at the cars as they passed.

None stopped all morning. The water was gone by noon, and the heat was already unbearable about two hours before that. His feet hurt and he was hungry. There was no gas station yet, nothing but the road, the sun, and the rocks. Soon he was limping and he was positive there were a couple of blisters working on each foot. No one stopped in the early afternoon. Growing weary and lightheaded, he finally sat down next to a barbed-wire fence and thought he might go no further. He didn't remember it being this far to the gas station they'd stopped at the day before. Frustrated, he began to cry. He contemplated walking out into traffic to stop somebody, telling them he thought he was nearing the line between life and death in his situation. He laughed maniacally. Would that even matter to anyone? They might not stop at all. Then there was the possibility that in his state he would misjudge the speed and distance and just get run over. That might not be so bad. He decided to reserve it as an option, but knowing his luck lately, he wouldn't even die. He'd probably remain conscious with a few broken bones and bleed to death waiting for an ambulance. Maybe then he could get some water.

He slowly became aware that the air around him was foul and oily. Looking up from between his knees, he saw a big rig idling on the shoulder, all white and shiny chrome, a mere fifteen feet in front of him. He hadn't heard the brakes. It was hauling several hundred large white turkeys stacked in tiny metal cages. Wiping his face on the back of his sleeve, he got up and limped over. The man had the passenger door open for him, and John climbed up gingerly, trying not to look feeble.

"Hey old-timer," the man said as John entered the cab and closed the door.

John nodded and put his bedding between his feet, then looked at the man. He was most certainly older than John, by at least a decade. He had a good-natured smile, which he displayed generously. His hair appeared all white under a John Deere cap, and he had a closely trimmed white beard.

"Hello, sir. Thank you."

"Don't sir me. Where you headed?" He still smiled.

"That way." John nodded ahead.

"Fair enough," the man said, and the truck heaved forward.

21

"Name's Dean. What's yours?"

John was drinking a bottle of water Dean had given him. "John," he said, wiping a drop from his chin, self-consciously. "Thank you for the water. And for picking me up."

"Pleased to meet you, John." Dean's hands were large, a bit shakey, and extremely wrinkled, but they handled the steering wheel gracefully.

"Likewise. You know I don't always get around like this."

"Of course not. And I don't usually pick up hitchhikers, what with the state of the world as it is, but you looked like you'd be okay. Had to exit and turn around to come back and get you, though."

"Well thank you for that. I hate to ask for anything else but I'm going to."

"Don't mention it. If I can help, I will, if I can't, I won't."

"Got any aspirin?"

"Glove-box."

John found the aspirin and put four in his mouth, swallowing them with the last swig of water.

"How do you usually travel?"

"I have a van, but it got stolen."

"No kidding. How'd that happen?"

"I picked up some hitchhikers, these two kids, called themselves rainbow people. They seemed nice enough. We had a picnic, and I fell asleep for a few minutes, I guess. When I woke up, they were gone, with my van and my wallet."

"Sorry to hear that. That's why I don't pick up hitchhikers." Dean chuckled. "You call the police?"

"Not yet. Hell, I'll probably never see it again, anyway. Probably not much use."

"Maybe not. Funny, that doesn't sound like something rainbow folks would do. Most of them are just old hippies, anyway. For the most part they're not bad people." After John looked at him, Dean added, "I have a much younger brother who goes to rainbow gatherings. Mostly him and his friends just camp out and smoke dope. He's kind of the black sheep. Only artist in a family of law enforcement officers, but he's a good ol' boy, mostly. Never done nothin' too terrible, aside from getting messed up on marijuana and mushrooms out in the middle of nowhere, so we just accept him like he is."

"You're in law enforcement? What are you doing driving around a trailer full of turkeys?"

"Retired. I was Sheriff of a little county in western Arizona for forty years. I can't bring myself to sit around and do nothin', and my wife's dead, so this is what I do now."

"Mind if I ask how old you are?"

"Nope. seventy-nine."

"My god, Dean, you're a tough bird, aren'tcha?"

"Men live a long time in my family."

"I'm sixty-six and dying of cancer."

"My wife died of the cancer. Not a day goes by that I don't miss her. How much longer they think you got?"

John laughed and coughed. "What day is it?"

"Just remember, John, you can always hang on longer. They don't really know too much, these doctors. They're good guessers, but even good guessers are wrong a lot. They gave Jeanie a year, and she made it four." He looked ahead at the road, but at something far in the distance that John knew he wouldn't be able to see. "But they were difficult years."

"I'm sure they were. I'm sorry to hear that." John sat thinking, and then added, "It's a hard life."

"Yes it is, my friend. Full of hardships, but also unimaginable beauty. Most of the time, it's really great and really hard all in the same breathe." He sighed. John wasn't sure, but he thought he might have cried a little. They sat in silence for some time, and Dean finally said, "Maybe we can call in your van at the next stop, have a trooper or somebody take down the description of these kids. You get names? I suppose they were fake, but maybe not."

"I'm pretty sure they were fake- Blossom was the guy, and Panera."

Dean started laughing. It made John slightly uncomfortable. Was he laughing at him?

"Those two are definitely not rainbow people, unless they just go to gatherings to try and steal stuff. They're just petty crooks. They operate around this area of the state. She turns tricks sometimes at truck stops when they're low on money and stealing isn't going well. Well, only with handsome, young guys...she still has some scruples, for the time being. She's a pretty thing isn't she?"

"She sure is." John felt stupid.

"For now- they're into meth, from what I hear, and that will not be forgiving for very long." Dean shook his head. "It's sad. Waste of beauty and maybe intelligence, although I'm not too sure about the latter, as I've never spoken with the lady."

"She's smart enough, I guess." John smiled.

"I'll tell you, the state of the world today…" Dean's voice drifted off and then he seemed to find his bearings. "Did you hear about those cops in Oklahoma? One of 'em shot the Fire Chief in their town?" John shook his head no, and Dean continued. "Little town, only a small handful of officers. They apparently didn't have enough to do, so they set up speed traps, gave tickets away like they were going out of style. Well it's a small town, and people start gettin angry. They all start complaining, it becomes a real problem. The Fire Chief goes to court to contest a ticket. Some of the officers are there for the hearing. The Chief leaves afterwards, gets caught in a trap on his way home. Gets another ticket. He goes back to the courthouse, angry as hell, and rightfully so, I would imagine, but I don't have all the details- and an argument ensues right there in the courthouse, an argument which ends with one of the officers shooting the Fire Chief in the back. In the dang back! Now he's in critical condition, may not live. There's an investigation, and it's found that these guys were writing tickets way outside their jurisdiction, and nobody can figure where all the money was going, most of it seems to have disappeared." He shook his head in disbelief. "They were running a racket in their own town, against the citizens they were sworn to protect. Only in Oklahoma…well maybe Texas, but goddamn. And to shoot that man as he's walking away. How does it come to that? I drew my firearm twelve times in my forty years as sheriff, and I fired it three times. I shot and killed one man. Missed the other times. I didn't draw it at all as a deputy, in the years prior. You ever in the service?"

"Yes."

"Nam?"

"Yes. Were you?"

"Korea. What were you, army?"

"Infantry."

"Me too."

"Do you think we'll go to hell for the people we killed?" John asked, surprising himself. Did he really just ask that?

Dean seemed to wonder, and then said, "Don't know. I hope not. Don't know for sure that there is a heaven or a hell. But I do know that if there is one, there's a lot of people that deserve to be there a lot more than you or me."

"Are you saying that about heaven or about hell?"

"Hell. But I guess both, now that you mention it," Dean said.

"Bible says you have to ask for forgiveness. Repent."

"Have you?"

"Yes."

"Do you think that's enough?"

"I don't know."

"Is it enough for you personally?"

John waited, then said, "I don't know."

"The Bible says a lot of things. I've studied in church my whole life, and am still perplexed by the contradictions. You've gotta remember that it was translated three or four times, words that meant one thing then don't mean the same thing now, and events weren't necessarily put to paper in some cases until centuries after

104

they were supposed to have occurred. But common sense has always told me that if you follow your inner voice, then you'll probably always know what's right, more or less, so if asking for forgiveness isn't good enough for you, how can you expect it to be good enough for God?"

"That's a good question," John said, feeling exhausted. "But isn't God's law absolute?"

"Supposedly, but if that book is how he's chosen to speak to us, then what does that tell you?"

"I should learn Hebrew?"

"You might want to throw in some Aramaic and definitely some Greek."

"I don't think I have time."

"Guess we've both got to trust the experts or fly blind. Neither is an ideal prospect, if you ask me."

22

Long after dark, Dean woke John and asked him if he wanted to stop for a beer and a burger. "This place has decent food. Not great, but I could sure use something. Don't worry, I don't mind paying for you."

John peered out the window, sleepily. He recognized the bar as the first place he had stopped to look for Bud White, only now the parking lot was full. "Hey, I've been here," he said. "Stopped on my way through." He didn't tell Dean he was feeling very sick and not hungry. If he started to eat, he hoped he might feel better.

Dean parked the truck at the end of the parking lot. They both exited, John leaving behind his bed on the floor.

"I'm gonna just take a leak over here, before I get inside and have to wait in line," John said, walking a few feet, and facing away from the lot.

"Sure, I'll get us a seat and some beer." Dean waved, and walked spryly towards the bar door.

John finished and zipped and turned around to go inside and was surprised to see a red, white and blue striped decal along the side of a white van. It looked just like his. The back stuck out from between two other cars. He walked over to it. It was his. He tried the back door. It opened. There was some crap belonging to the kids, a dirty backpack, some clothes, Panera's Scooby Doo panties balled up, empty fast food wrappers.

One of his extra blankets was still folded neatly in a corner by the spare tire. He slid his hand between the folds, feeling slowly, and drew out the pistol. It was still loaded. He stuck it in the back of his pants, shut the door as softly as he could, and headed inside.

It was busy. The small establishment had three pocket-sized rooms, crowded wall to wall with bodies and smoke, but Dean had somehow grabbed two seats at the bar. John passed by him like a spectre and searched for Blossom and Panera. The room with the pool tables didn't have anyone that wasn't playing pool, and they weren't among them. He walked through that until he got to the last segment of the building, where the kitchen seemed to be, and another, smaller bar with about six stools. He saw them in a booth, under a yellow lamp. They were huddled together, talking with some biker guy.

John walked up behind Blossom without being noticed. As he pulled out the gun, the biker's drunken eyes honed in on it and he leapt up and clumsily jumped over the back of the booth and ran into the kitchen, knocking over a dishwasher. He disappeared, but the sound of his escape lingered behind the swinging door, as if half the kitchen were tumbling down as he tried to find a back exit. Panera stared at John, stunned and silent as he stuck the pistol into Blossom's head, just above his neck.

"Gimme my keys, you stinky bastard." Blossom turned his head around, confused and very drunk. John pistol-whipped him across the brow and slammed his face to the table. A woman screamed and some people tried to run away, but it was too dark to see much of anything. The background noise of the bar still hung in the air like a static atmosphere, soupy wet and heavy. "Give em to me," he repeated.

"Mister, I told him it was a bad idea, I told him it was wrong," Panera blurted out, crying.

"Shut-up. Just give 'em to me."

"They're in his pocket."

"So get 'em for me." She did, shaking so much she almost dropped them.

"Where's my wallet?"

"It's in the car."

"Where is it?" he asked again, not hearing well.

"It's in your car. We just used it to buy food. We still have a little of our own money."

"Ok. You have a nice day. Stay off the meth, kids. It'll ruin your beautiful figure."

"I will. I promise." she said, her bottom lip trembling.

John patted her head and put his gun back under his shirt and walked out the front door without looking at anyone. He sat on a broken wooden step at the end of a long porch, trying not to pass out, and waited for the cops. He put the pistol between his feet. The biker must have found a back exit because he was now in the parking lot getting his chopper started. He gunned the hell out of it and slid out as he turned the corner onto the street. John could hear him swearing and kicking his bike, and then he must have decided to leave it, because he saw him running across the highway into the darkness. A few other people were also leaving and staring at John, but not as many as he would have thought.

The door opened again and someone walked over. He figured it was Dean. He looked up, trying to get his mind to organize some kind of explanation, but he was surprised to see the bartender woman he had spoken with earlier in the week.

"I can't believe you're here again," she said.

"I can't believe it either."

"I saw the man you were looking for, two nights ago. He must have come in for a drink. I didn't see him until he was leaving, but it was the guy. I followed him outside and he drove off in an old Chevy truck. He was going

108

east. I didn't get the license plate, but I called the cops. I don't think they found him." She suddenly seemed to notice the gun on the ground. "Oh my gosh. Did you start that fight?"

John got up without saying anything and walked unsteadily to his van. He stashed the piece under the seat. He drove toward home and expected the police to stop him, but none did. Over an hour passed without so much as a siren.

Bud must have tried to go visit his family and then decided to backtrack. He had friends near Entierro. Perhaps he meant to lay low there for a while. Maybe he was turning himself in, or maybe he only came through here and then took off north or south.

John felt bad about leaving without saying goodbye to Dean, but staying probably wasn't a good idea, even if he was just trying to get his van back. He looked at the gas gage. He would need to stop and get some before long, so he hoped Panera wasn't lying and his card still had money on it. The wallet was in one of the cup holders, what looked like ketchup splattered across.

A flapping noise suddenly began to rise from the road. A tire was loosing air. He pulled over to the shoulder and got out. The entire passenger-side bumper and wheel well were crushed inward. He hadn't noticed it earlier, but the kids must have hit something. The tire was now totally flat. In the glare of the headlights against the moonless night, he could see what looked like copper wire fraying from the damaged metal. He rubbed it between his fingers. It was soft, but slightly coarse. He pulled it free in a clump. It was wet. Holding it directly in the light, he saw it was bloody animal hair.

He went to the back of the van and found the jack in the spare tire. He put the jack aside and tried to lift the spare, but it was too heavy for him. He was exhausted and shivering again with fever. He tried once more, and couldn't get it. Finally, he heaved with every ounce of strength he had left, pulled it free and almost fell over backwards. Letting it bounce to the ground, he started to roll it around to the front. Just as he reached the passenger side he tripped on something, maybe his own foot, and went over the tire, landing head first against the road. He grabbed his skull in pain, seeing white spots until the blood ran into his eyes. He sat up with his back to the truck and then slowly drooped over, unconscious.

23

Somewhere down the line was Dale Podobinski. And the girl. They were there like a luminous gray fog, stretching permanently across a dimpled black ocean, impossible to see through, yet out of necessity he would always need to.

Dale was a quiet kid, only eighteen years old, from somewhere called Buttermilk, Kansas. He was actually a few months in when it happened, but he was still greener than hell. He was what they called born green. It was a sad, ugly color to be where they were. John liked him. He was a good guy, nice, thoughtful, and shy. But good guy or not, if you were born green you were a liability. No one wanted to be around him because they were afraid he was going to do something stupid and get them killed. They called him Pody. He was scared half to death of everything. He cried almost daily, which annoyed the hell out of everyone. Not only did you have to worry about him getting you dead, you had to listen to him blubber and moan. Podobinski was simply not cut out for where he was, which was why John was so surprised by what happened.

He remembered the air that morning. It was clear, fresh, and slightly charged with electricity, as if it was going to rain. Even though it was teaming with life, the jungle felt peaceful as the platoon walked single file across the edge of a long rice paddy field, towards a village they were going to search for about the fifth time and probably end up burning, no matter what. They pretty well knew those fuckers were VC, but couldn't prove it. Someplace near was a major supply store, and the village had to be it. There was nowhere else. Though they'd searched it before, nobody really knew where to look or what to look for. They would poke around in some rice baskets, blow a couple of them with a grenade or two, get yelled at by the villagers, and then leave.

This time would be different. They would find the ammo stores, and if they didn't, they'd burn it all to the ground for good measure, just like the last three villages. There had been way too much activity in the region lately, too many lives lost, and that was the way it was going to be. Time to break some eggs and save some lives.

As they came up out of a small meadow on the other side of the paddy field and were about to re-enter the tree line, still some three miles south of the village, someone yelled from behind John. They were taking fire from across the area they'd just traversed. Someone fell hard, and a bullet zipped close to John's head. Everybody dropped. The grass was nearly five feet tall. Someone was screaming in pain. Then a couple of people were screaming in pain. It sounded like one of them was Cole Evans. Moses Vasquez was next to John, and Butch Collins was just a little closer to the trees. Lieutenant Roberts could be heard yelling from up front to get into the trees quickly for cover. Those who were already in the relative safety of the canopy were firing blindly across the field.

Their medic, Carl, came slithering down the muddy grass between them and asked John and Moses to go help him find out who was hurt. Butch gratefully took the opportunity to crouch and run up into cover. The whizzing sound of bullets were everywhere. The other three crawled through the grass on their bellies for about fifteen feet until they came to Evans and Dale Podobinksi. Pody was crouched down, shaking and crying. Evans was

112

on his side, pale and in shock, breathing heavily and bleeding profusely from his crotch.

John put his hand on Pody's shoulder. "Who else was back here? Wasn't Sanders back here?" Pody put his head between his hands and started rocking back and forth. There was a deafening crack from the tree line and black muddy earth rained down. The four of them jolted and ducked. John heard somebody yell about mortars. It definitely wasn't a random sniper. There was a succession of explosions, each falling in the general direction of the forest. More fire. Then more booming that rattled John's chest cavity and made him feel hollow. Moses grunted. John looked at him. He was spitting out pieces of his own bloody teeth into cupped hands.

"Aww Fucthh," he said. "Fucthh!"

"Shit. Hang on," Carl said, fumbling through his kit. Evans lay bleeding to death.

Moses kept saying, "Fucthh."

"Take a look at 'em, John." Carl said into an eerie, brief silence. Then the chaotic noise returned.

Moses was freaking out. He was now clawing at his mouth and screaming, broken bits of tooth and blood dripping down his forearms. John tried to pull his arms away to look, but wasn't able. He yelled to Pody for help, but Pody was petrified with fear, trembling like a puppy in a thunderstorm. It was exactly what John felt like doing. He noticed his own hands were shaking.

He was able to stop them by finally pinning Moses down, but it wasn't easy. Moses' head thrashed from side to side and the veins in his neck bulged. John thought he saw something small lodged in his mandible, between an entire front row of shattered pearly whites. A big gash split his bottom lip.

"Shrapnel, I think," John said.

"Can you pull it out?"

"He's gonna bite my fucking hand off if I put it in there."

"Try!" Carl was putting pressure on Evans' wound, which he had cut the fabric away from to expose. It was as if an oil well of blood had sprung beneath Evans' ass.

Almost quicker than the eye could follow, as if they were choreographed wrestlers sparring, John let go of one of Moses' arms and stuck his fingers in his mouth. Moses immediately gripped John's shoulder with a hard pinch. He didn't try to throw him off, but he did start to bite down reflexively. John let go of the other arm and was ready to pry his upper jaw. Moses frantically grabbed at John with his now free arm and John whispered soothingly, "Hold on now, c'mon, let me see if I can help, c'mon …" over and over like a prayer while Moses whined and growled, high pitched and frightened. Slowly, with intense difficulty, Moses was able to open his mouth and John felt for metal in the red mess, but now couldn't distinguish between the organic or the man made intruder.

Suddenly Carl was hunched over the two of them with some kind of pliers, and he stuck them in and tapped around gently, sending Moses into conniptions. Carl screamed at John to hold him down, so John leaned his whole weight into him, and the two of them held his head still while Carl tapped around some more, then clasped the fulcrum and yanked out a piece of metal about an inch long, holding it to the sky and smiling like a sadistic dentist.

They lay down on either side of Moses for a moment, panting like exhausted lovers. Moses stared at the sky as if just waking from a dream. Dirt continued to fly from the exploding mortar rounds.

"Can we try and get out of here?" John nodded in the direction of Evans, who was unconscious.

114

"Yeah, you and I can drag him in. I slowed the bleeding." Carl looked at Moses and asked, "Can you get yourself back to those trees?" But Moses was already turned and running before he finished. In a flash he was gone, his M-16 hanging from his right hand, his left cupped over his bloody mouth. "Shit. Pody." Dale looked up sheepishly. "You've gotta get up ahead and make sure we get cover fire. We're gonna bring in Evans. We can't count on Moses to remember. He's probably in shock and I don't know if he can talk, anyway. Can you do that? It's either that, or you've gotta let John go, then you and me bring him in slow. I'd take door number one if I was you."

Pody nodded. He positioned himself to go.

"Hold on," John said. "I'll crawl over there aways and cover you. When I fire, you go."

"Ok," Pody said, and then, "Wait. Why don't you two just carry him right now, and I'll walk behind you, and provide cover from your backs? All that other maneuvering may just make us more vulnerable. What do you think?"

"Let's do it. Sooner we're out of this grass, the better," Carl said.

"Right," John said. He almost volunteered to switch places with him and be the one to get shot at. John had more experience, but this seemed to be a turning point for Pody, and so he let him have it. Besides, it was more the illusion of safety. Neither of them would be able to see jack shit running backwards through tall grass. He and Carl each cupped one of Evan's armpits, and they shouted, "Go!" and were off.

The rest of the platoon saw them coming and layed on the firepower over their heads. In a few seconds they were up into the relative safety of tree cover, but it appeared they were fighting off an attack from within the jungle as well. John saw many more wounded and dead. He turned around and was happy to see Dale alive, panting behind him.

Within minutes, an air strike Lieutenant Roberts had called in fire bombed the tree line across the meadow, in a welcomed spectacle of orange napalm hell. By the end of the hour, they had killed every gook they could find, and were tending to the wounded. Out of the thirty-seven men who had begun the hump that day, there were eleven dead and Mike Sanders was still missing. Another five were hurt too bad to continue, bringing the total now down to twenty.

Almost another hour passed, and some of the guys divided the dead men's dope and smoked it while they waited for the choppers to carry them away. Pody sat silently with the other men. They passed the joint around him. He was covered in blood like everyone else. That afternoon he had finally become a killing machine. John remembered wondering if it would last.

They were given the option to go back to base camp and call it a day, but nobody wanted to. Lieutenant Roberts led them to the village to destroy it. They didn't even look for a weapons stash. They walked up and started shooting all the livestock, chickens, pigs, and dogs. A water buffalo was hitched to a rickety old wagon, so Ben Foster threw a grenade in the back and the noise sent it running through the village. When it passed John, he could see a chunk of flesh was blown out of its left hindquarter. A few villagers tried to stop it and one got run over, his body left broken and mangled in a cloud of dust. The people cried and screamed and surrounded his limp form, but were held back and dragged away by the soldiers. Someone shot the buffalo out of either pity or rage and someone else laughed and remarked that the man's ear was flattened and smeared to its hoof as if it were a dead leaf.

They went from hut to hut, either blowing them out with grenades, or just lighting them on fire. Every basket of rice was blown. Despite not trying to find anything, they did stumble upon a tunnel in an old well at the edge of the village and blew it out. They didn't find any bodies, but they found a very small stash of weapons. The villagers said the VC made them keep the guns by threat of force, and it was force that now removed them from their homes. If they ever had the means to return, they would find nothing. By the time they left that day, not a single soldier had a grenade or anti-personnel mine left.

As John made his way to the center of the village, lighting a cigarette and everything dry enough to burn with his Zippo, he saw Pody in one of the huts with his pants down, raping a young girl. She was probably fourteen or so, but it was hard to tell. She wasn't fighting back, at least anymore. Her face was broken open and swollen and she was barely conscious. John was so shocked he just stood and looked, expecting the image before him to correct itself somehow.

"What the hell are you doing?" he finally said. "Get outta there Dale." He shut his lighter with a click and pocketed it. Dale turned his head for an instant, but didn't stop. He kept humping his skinny white hips like his life depended on it.

"C'mon, buddy, let's go. Move it." He moved toward him and grabbed Dale's shoulder, but Dale shrugged him off and kept at it. With one swift jolt of his body, John cracked him square in the head with the butt of his rifle, but he hit him much harder than he meant to. Or maybe he meant to. Either way, Dale went down fast and started to have some kind of seizure. Within moments he stopped moving and white foam was bubbling from his mouth. One finger kept twitching for a few more seconds, as if he were tapping out his frantic last thoughts in Morse code.

"Shit." John felt for a pulse, but it was already gone. "You fucking asshole." Dale stared back with unmoving eyes. John looked around. He didn't know what to do. Should he give him CPR? Nobody was in eyesight. He looked at the girl. She sat still, facing the wall of the small hut, naked from the waist down. Blood was smeared between her legs and she had a large cut above her right eye. "Go on," he said. "Get out of here." She didn't move or acknowledge him in any way. "Xin chao," he tried again. She stayed.

John rose from kneeling and wandered outside. The sun was disappearing behind long, dark, gunmetal clouds. A gust of wind stung the slope of the elevated village, causing those huts already burning to shoot flames sideways and then downward, singeing the ground. John tried to take a drag from his smoke, but it was gone. He walked to a neighboring hut and flicked his Zippo, but his thumb wouldn't work. He went to the next one and couldn't do it either. He heard voices yelling as if slowly oozing through a torn hole from another dimension. He turned to see Blake Turner and Mavis Washington standing at the hut's entrance. They pulled the girl out by her hair and called her a stupid bitch and a murderer. They didn't seem to notice she was half naked. Mavis stood her up and punched her in the face. John couldn't let them know he killed Dale, so he stood and watched, shaking his head and muttering to himself as Blake cocked his rifle back and executed her with a bullet to the head. Her frail body crumpled like paper.

John continued watching them. They now seemed to be taking in the scene more completely. Dale's pants around his ankles, his bloody dingus hanging like a dead worm, her bare legs.

"What the hell happened here?" Mavis asked.

"He was raping her," John said, walking over.

"What? Well holy crap," said Blake. "Did you see it?"

"No, but what else could've happened?"

"Pody's a rapist? Naw."

"What else? Didn't you see any of this before you shot her?"

"It's been a hard day, John. I don't know what I saw. I guess I just thought she shot him or something."

"So she killed him while he was raping her?" Mavis asked himself and the group in general. "How? She's so small. Maybe he just keeled over dead."

"Maybe," John said. "But it's too late to ask her."

Mavis and Blake looked at each other. "Shit," Blake said. "We could get in trouble for this."

"You could, white boy. You shot her," Mavis clarified.

"Goddamnit!" Blake kicked her legs furiously. He looked at the two bodies as if he'd just backed his car into a mailbox. "We could just pack him up and leave."

"Better pull his pants up," Mavis recommended.

"Alright, let's do it," Blake said, frantically. "You guys put that skirt thing back on her."

"You do it. You shot the poor bitch," Mavis backed off.

"And you decked her, asshole."

John picked up her skirt and draped it over her torso and legs. "Get Dale quick. Let's get outta here." He started to walk away.

"What are we gonna say happened to him?"

John stopped. "Say you found him like that." He looked at Mavis. "I'd help him if I was you. Get that boy's pants up. Get him outta here."

"John, don't say nothin'."

"I ain't sayin' nothin'."

"You sure? 'Cuz you're kind of a softie at heart. You sure your conscience ain't gonna get the better of you later on?"

"It won't. It was a mistake. Let's bury it and leave." He left them and kept burning huts.

Soon they were joined by reinforcements to help deal with the few villagers who'd resisted and been killed or injured, and lead them all away from their burning homes to an interim camp. John scooped up a small boy left alone in the confusion. He was maybe four years old. Each clung tight to the other.

The soldiers forcefully escorted the former residents away from the village, captor and captive alike all filthy and ragged and stumbling one after the other, dazed, like some ancient brethren who lost their order's purpose, their scrolls crumbled to dust, their new mantra recorded in the frenzied bloody footpaths they left behind.

On the hump back they spotted a person hanging from a tree by the river about a half-mile ahead, silhouetted against an endless stormy sky. Roberts lost his binoculars somewhere earlier that day, but by the time they got within one hundred meters they knew it was Ike Sanders. He hung naked, his genitals hacked off and stuffed in his mouth. Stuck to his chest was a note that said, *Screw Jakie Robinsin*. It was the end of one mystery.

"Fuckers," muttered Mavis, his head down in solemn regard for his dead companion.

They cut his stiffening body loose and started again. John looked at the face of the boy he carried for the first time and saw nothing he could recognize. It almost gave him a panic attack, but he stayed focused on his task and moved forward methodically, shifting the child to his other hip every half mile or so. By the time he left him at transport with the other villagers, on a thin dirt road carved like a scar into the lush countryside, his brief episode was over and human faces looked normal to him.

120

Or he was just numb again. It was hard to tell. He gave the boy a chocolate bar and watched as he boarded the truck to the new refugee camp. No one had really claimed him, but an old woman patted him on the head like she may have known him. He looked back at John with sad eyes. John wondered what would become of him, then suddenly wanted to run up to the truck and take him and move far away from everything. He turned and left, refusing to look at the child any longer.

At camp that night the rain poured out of the darkness in hard grey sheets, like a thousand rivers flowing straight from the sky. Blake grew antsy and said he was going to pray with the chaplain. It was something he never did. John smoked three joints and drank half a bottle of whiskey and listened to the rain, a white noise temporarily claiming the world. He went outside to stand in it for a while, wondering if he could drown just from looking up and opening his mouth. Drunk, he lurched to the edge of camp and chucked his empty bottle into the trees. No one bothered him. Later he found Moses' stash of tranquilizer pills and took one before bed. He passed out soaking wet.

In the morning the girl's face was still in his head as if burned into the woven fabric of his consciousness, and though the guilt over his silence would slowly fade with time like the aging of a garment, her image would always be there, faint and soft, whispering and laughing like a bored ghost.

24

John woke in a hospital or institution of some sort. Mello's head hovered above him like a genie from some kids' TV show.

It said, "You got fired from Pearl's for disappearing. Your cats are mad at you. Merlin peed on your bed." John tried swatting it away. "Hey, he's awake! He just moved his hand."

John passed out again and woke later, more coherent, to see Mello and Aubrey standing, and a woman sitting in a chair next to the door. She looked familiar. He tried to raise his head, but hadn't the strength. He felt confused. Even the hair on his head hurt.

The woman stood up anxiously. Her hands cradled themselves, and she took a step closer to the bed. "Hello, Johnny," It was Caroline, his sister. She looked much the same to him all of a sudden. He just wasn't used to seeing her.

He tried to answer, but could barely speak. After clearing his throat, he answered hoarsely, "Hey Carrie. What are you doing here?"

"I came to see you."

"That's nice of you."

"Your cats are mad at you," Mello chimed in. "Merlin peed on your bed."

Aubrey elbowed him. "C'mon, let's let him talk to his sister." They left them alone.

"Your friends are nice."

"They're ok, aren't they? Carmello's a little daft, but I'm sure you could tell. But he's not as dumb as he looks or sounds." He coughed.

"They were worried about you."

"I'm ok. What am I doing here?"

"You've got pneumonia. You passed out changing a tire on the highway. A state trooper found you."

John wondered how he would tell her the rest.

"What's that, hon'?" She sat down next to the bed and rested her hand on his.

"Oh. Was I talking just then?"

"You were mumbling a little."

"Oh. It's worse than that." Despite himself, he started to cry. He hardly had the energy. He wiped his face with the back of his arm. "I've got cancer, Carrie. It's eating me up. I'm gonna die soon."

"Oh, Johnny, I know." She grabbed his hand and squeezed. She started to cry as well.

"I'm sorry," he said.

"Sorry for what, honey?"

"Making you cry."

"It's ok."

25

Caroline stayed with John, allowing Aubrey and Mello to return home to work. The pair had driven together from Entierro once they'd located him. After nearly a week had gone by without any word, Mello started checking John's answering machine every day for clues. They actually thought he'd gone off somewhere to kill himself. It turned out he was in a minor coma at a hospital in Gallup. The hospital located his phone number through his driver's license and called looking for a next of kin.

Mello knew John recently communicated with his sister, and tore apart what was left of his house after the cats had their run of things, located her letter, and retrieved her phone number from the internet. Caroline dropped everything and flew down from Minnesota, beating them there.

John convinced them all he hadn't tried to kill himself, that he'd just passed out on the side of the road on his way home from camping. He was beyond embarrassed, but couldn't think about it too much because he was so sick. Aubrey and Mello promised to come back soon.

Caroline stayed at a hotel a couple of miles away, and arrived every morning at nine. She stayed until about eight o'clock most nights. She chatted with all the hospital staff cheerfully, and always made sure they were paying enough attention to him.

John liked having her around. They talked about the old days a little, about when their mom disappeared, and how hard it must have been on their father. John allowed that he'd managed to forgive him a little for being such a hard-ass after he learned of his passing. He and little Petey, the middle brother, had gotten the worst of it, Carrie agreed. But she and Stephanie didn't exactly have a free ride, she reminded him. He asked about how they both were doing. She didn't talk to either one of them very often. They were both divorced.

"Neither one came to Dad's funeral," she said. "Only me."

"I'm sorry you had to take care of everything. If I'd known, maybe…"

"You still probably wouldn't have made it," she laughed.

"Well, I don't know."

"Remember that time you and Dad got into that fist fight on the kitchen floor?" she asked, smiling a little.

"Yes. Thanks for reminding me."

"Sorry. You know he really loved you. He loved all of us. He just did the best he could."

"Yeah, I suppose."

"Remember that package he sent to you when you were overseas?"

"What package?"

"The one you sent back, unopened."

"Yes."

"I remember the day it came back. I got home from school and it was sitting outside. I almost took it and hid it. But I didn't. He never said anything when he got home. But it was gone by dinner."

John suddenly felt trapped. He didn't want to talk about this anymore. "Yeah, well, he was an asshole before I left, and I didn't have time for that shit over there." They both sat silent for a minute.

"I'm sorry for mentioning that."

"Do you know what was in it?"

"No, you know him. He didn't talk about stuff like that."

"Yeah. Stoic old bastard."

It felt good to see her. She was so nice to him, almost motherly. She told him her daughter was pregnant with her first grandbaby, six months along. She called her husband every day for updates, and told John about every detail when he was awake, as if he were really part of the family. She said she'd missed him all those years he'd been gone. He cried when she told him that. But mostly he just slept.

His pneumonia was bacterial, and to everyone's surprise, he responded incredibly well to the antibiotics. Within two weeks he was nearly over it. He gave the credit to Caroline. It was as if her mere presence radiated life force. It felt like she was giving something new to him, that he couldn't explain. Maybe it was just hope. The overall picture was still the same. He was dying, but it wasn't yet time, although it could really be anytime, the doctor said. He felt a strange sense of peace about his few remaining days, and wanted very much to go home and begin chemotherapy again with the hope that he could hang on a little longer. Perhaps he would be able to meet this baby. He decided he wanted that. Deep down he held onto a small feeling that maybe he could still beat this thing. Maybe a miracle was possible, but it was such a small feeling, nothing more than a whisper, that he didn't dare utter it for fear of it leaving like a butterfly being chased by a child.

126

Soon he was strong enough to travel and Aubrey came back to give him a ride home. His van was still impounded and he didn't have the money to get it out, so they decided to leave it. He was hoping to sell his house, but it had fallen in value with the rest of the housing market, and he hadn't made his last mortgage payment. Aubrey was going to give him a job for seven dollars an hour answering phones and running the register at the shop, and even though John knew it was charity, he reluctantly agreed to take it.

John was worried about the hospital stay, because his veteran's health insurance didn't cover much. Caroline told him not to worry about it, that if she had to, she and her husband could take care of things. After she said that, he didn't voice his concerns, because it was wrong that she would have to take care of any of this, his life's catastrophe. She made him promise to call regularly with updates on his progress. John wanted to joke that he'd probably keep progressing toward death at an accelerated rate, but he didn't say it.

Aubrey and he drove home seven hours straight. John slept through most of it. Aubrey took special pride in being able to drive long distances without stopping to sleep. He patted John on the shoulder to wake him when they got to his house.

John walked slowly to the porch and leaned heavily on the guardrail. That was enough to nearly exhaust him. He got up the steps, taking Aubrey's hand for the last one. John bent over slowly and fumbled to flip the mat and get the key. Aubrey put out his hand and took it from him, for which John was secretly grateful, and got the door open quickly.

"Hello, my beauties!" John called into the quiet house. Pirouette came rushing out of the darkness and slammed into his leg, rubbing her head against him passionately. Merlin was absent.

"Bonnie cleaned up the place a little, because we all know Mello's not too good at that. And I don't know if you remember, but Merlin peed on your bed, so she also changed the sheets and mostly got the smell out." Aubrey grinned.

"Tell her thank you for me, so much, Aubrey. Really."

"She's happy to do it. She left some dinner in the fridge and a few more in the freezer. Just bring the Tupperware to the shop when you report to work. When do you want to start, later in the week?"

"Tomorrow, if it's ok."

"You sure? Don't overdo it. You can come in whenever you want. Old Jay's only part time, but Charlie and I can cover it till then. It'll be nice to not have to worry about the phones anymore."

"Charlie's back?"

"He is. He's feeling better."

"Good. He's a good kid."

"Yeah. He's not the same, but he's doing better."

"It takes time." John thought about telling Aubrey what he'd heard from the bartender woman, but decided it wasn't worth it. She probably hadn't seen Bud White, anyway. All the same, he thought maybe he'd call the sheriff's office in the morning. "I'll see you tomorrow."

"Tomorrow it is." Aubrey patted his shoulder and shuffled down the steps to his truck.

As John shut the door, Merlin appeared from somewhere and savagely attached himself to his leg, biting down. John yelped, kicking his leg frantically. He heard Pirouette knocking something over in the kitchen. Merlin let go and meowed wildly, looking up and flicking his tail. "Welcome home, dad," John said, flipping on the light switch. "You guys hungry or what?"

128

26

He thought about calling the sheriff the next day to alert him of his possible Bud White sighting, but then realized he'd have to explain himself, and explaining himself at this point seemed like drinking turpentine to piss on a brushfire. Vengeance would come through the proper channels or maybe it wouldn't come at all, but it was time to live what was left of his life.

Eating breakfast, showering, toileting, feeding the cats and shaving his beard were enough to make him not ever want to move again. He took a puff off the inhaler the hospital had given him, ironed one of his nice flannel shirts, and finished getting dressed.

When he opened his front door Martin greeted him, happily wagging his tail. He bent down to pat him. Martin licked his face and hands and sniffed him deep in the chest.

"Don't wreck my shirt, I just ironed it, slobber face."

Martin walked with him to The Next Wave. They stopped halfway and John took another puff off the inhaler. When he got there Martin made himself comfortable outside the front entrance, laying down and sneezing three times.

John said hi to Aubrey and Charlie, and Aubrey showed him the cash register in front and gave him a very brief description of how to ring someone up. Then he brought him through a small door and down a step to his desk/garbage heap in the office, a tomb of decrepit fake wood paneling covered in a soft, mossy layer of dust.

"You'll spend most of your time in here. If someone pulls up for gas, it trips a little sensor and makes a dinging noise to let you know. The front door has a bell on it too. Coffee machine's in the corner there. Just brewed a pot this morning. Can't find the phone just yet, but when it rings, should be easy enough." Aubrey waved a hand generically at the dirty room, as if to prove its ability to swallow a phone. John imagined it harbored a few more treasures than that. It looked like it hadn't been disturbed in decades. "When you do find it you're welcome to take it outside and sit in a lawn chair like Jay does. It's cordless."

"You clean this place since your father died?"

"And get rid of all the good mojo? No way. Nothing but the occasional sweeping or litter patrol. There's the desk. Don't get lost. I've gotta get back to work. Let me know if you have any questions."

John sat behind the desk in a creaky chair, dry yellow foam bursting from split faux leather and crumbling to the floor like dehydrated cheese. He could have fallen asleep immediately if it wasn't for the rank stench of old chewing tobacco. A little investigating revealed that a whole row of coke cans along the edge of a window that looked into the shop doubled as Old Jay's spittoons. He managed to toss them out without gagging. By the end of the hour, he did doze off briefly, but the phone woke him with a loud video game style ringing. He found it underneath an enormous pile of receipts. It only rang three times all morning, and each time he had to excuse himself and go ask Aubrey the answer to the question on the other end of the line. About half a dozen people bought gas, and the first few times he also had to get Aubrey to show him how to use the cash register again.

Then it was lunchtime, and Charlie went to buy sandwiches.

They ate together in the office, mostly in silence. John felt bad that Aubrey had to eat lunch with one dying man and another who was essentially a widower, but he appeared to take it in stride. He made occasional conversation about some piece of news, car they were working on, or ornery customer, then pleasantly continued eating, seemingly at ease with the silence as it descended again and again over their meal.

John got bored after lunch, so he poked around in the desk for something to play with and found a stale cigarette amid an entire drawer of pens with no ink. He rolled it between his fingers and sniffed it, then rolled it some more, then slowly crumbled it to pieces over the trashcan. Just thinking about that smoke made his head hurt the rest of the day, but he suffered quietly until he found a bottle of Ibuprofen under an old baseball glove. He took four.

Charlie went home at six o'clock. John had been given the option to leave at five or even earlier if he wanted, but stayed because there wasn't anything to do at home but think about the future. He loved his cats, but they couldn't distract him like work, and that was what he wanted most. To keep busy until Aubrey left at seven, he swept the office and the concrete slab outside the front door, shooing Martin away briefly, and threw away every empty candy wrapper he could find, which itself took almost an hour. In the process he found an unopened Snickers bar and had it for a snack.

When Aubrey wandered in from the garage at ten of seven, covered in grease and grime, he went right to where John found the snickers bar, on top of a filing cabinet, and asked about it. John admitted to eating it and apologized, but Aubrey just waved him off and went to the small cooler in the corner and grabbed another one. There looked to be about twenty in there, piled over a six-pack of Miller Light, but John still felt like he'd stolen it. He didn't think anyone would bury a snack under a pile of empty wrappers, but apparently Aubrey knew it was there.

Aubrey offered him a ride home, but John declined. It was such a short walk. Aubrey showed him how to lock up and then left, his truck rolling across the gravel and onto the road as Martin slowly rose and shook out the willies to follow John home. Halfway there John had to stop and rest. He used the inhaler, but it didn't help much, so he sat down and cried and leaned on Martin, squeezing his coarse, thick fur. Martin licked his ear. After about ten minutes they continued.

27

John began Chemotherapy for the second time that year. He finally got summoned to court for his drug charges and then got them dropped because he didn't have any available life to pay the state back with, even if he was convicted. The whole mess took up too much time and he still had a few fees he could probably never pay, but Mello drove him to court for all of his appearances, and that was at least sort of entertaining.

Mello got a job tending bar at a new sports-themed-restaurant-mega-plex called Bust 'Em Down Barn!!!, which was located halfway to Albuquerque, in the middle of nowhere. It was shaped like an enormous, cartoon-red barn. It had an arcade, a bowling alley, four bars, three kitchens, six dining rooms, a miniature golf course, and fifty-six flat screen televisions, positioned everywhere, even over the urinals. People came from all over to play games or watch sports and get drunk and gorge themselves on goopy nachos.

This job became everything to Carmello. It was strange because he normally had a very extreme, unhealthy aversion to anything corporate that bordered on fanatic paranoia, but this new job didn't appear to bother him in the least. He talked about it constantly to anyone who would listen, which meant John most of the time, because Mello usually drove him to his Chemo treatments as well. He even mentioned the possibility of moving into management some day. There was apparently a lot of opportunity for advancement. He must have said to John at least four times, "I can't be a pot dealer forever. I mean it's glamorous and all, but someday I've gotta start looking ahead. Start thinking about raising a family."

The thought of Mello trying to raise a bunch of kids didn't strike John as very plausible, but it didn't bother him at first, listening to him babble on and on. Not like he thought it would. He was too sick most of the time to really care anyway, and actually it was kind of nice, listening to someone who was so excited about something. It gave him an odd sense of calm.

Laura started bringing John homemade dinner a couple of times a week, and he looked forward to her visits more than anything. She brought over soups and roasts and pies in Tupperware containers, and she would touch him affectionately with a soft hand and fuss over him. He felt bad because he couldn't always eat, but once in awhile she stayed for dinner and then he would eat more. On nights when he wasn't too tired, they had nice conversations about life, their deceased parents, and about how Charlie was coping. One night John expressed that he thought Charlie was doing great at work, and he seemed to be coming around, even though the latter wasn't really the case. He focused hard on work but seemed as down as ever.

Laura would entertain no illusions. "Something's changed in him, and it's not better yet. I don't know if he'll ever be the same."

"It's a hard blow, but it happened recently. He'll be ok, he's a tough kid."

Dinner was over and she sat on his couch, one leg tucked under her like a flamingo and the other extended across the cushions, both cats sprawled along either side of her long thigh. Their bellies faced upward, and each of her hands rubbed a swath of purring fur. John sat across, in his chair, watching her as if she were some primordial secret of happiness, on display in the showroom of a fevered dream. Vibrating and glowing. The feeling was sensual, yet not sexual and did not keep him from sharing in her remorse and her sadness. It was such a foggy sensation at times, dying the way he was. Not to make light of it, but half the time he didn't know if he was coming or going. There were moments when it was as if all life was pulling away from him and the only thing connecting him to what was solid and real were thin micro-strands of silk, like a spider's web, and he could feel the million light-years between two particles of dust, and the near infinite space between he and her, two galaxies, one fading and one shining on.

"I was able to protect him from his father all those years. I was always able to keep the abuse directed more or less at me, and was mostly able to hide it. And now what I've always feared seems to have happened anyway. Life's broken him and there's nothing I can do about it. I can't hide it, or take it away. It's so hard for me to accept that." A tear fell down either side of her face and she wiped each with a quick hand and went back to petting the cats. She smiled at John and he leaned forward and patted her on the knee. Pirouette batted his hand playfully.

"It really will be ok. It has to," he said.

"Does it? I hope you're right. I'm sorry, I'm supposed to be taking care of you. You're the sick one."

"We can all take care of each other."

She stayed for a while and they watched *Roman Holiday* on John's VCR. John fell asleep sometime before the end and Laura woke him. He was so tired and weak that she had to help him to bed. As they walked down the hall to his room Merlin leaped at them and she hissed at him and he scurried around the corner. She took off his shoes and pulled the blanket up.

28

John lost more weight. He was down to a hundred and forty-five pounds. His pants were too big for him now, but he couldn't afford to buy new ones. It seemed like he was always sick from the chemo and never fully rested. He forgot to feed the cats for two days until Merlin bit him. He missed a lot of work and when he was there he kept messing up and sometimes he could tell Aubrey was annoyed. It wasn't that he kept falling asleep, because Old Jay did that a lot too. It was just the mistakes. One week he made the wrong change about a half dozen times and cost the business money. Another time he was sent out to get sandwiches for lunch and forgot what he was doing and had to come back. Then he was too tired to go out again, so Charlie had to go.

He had a recurring nightmare in which he found himself alone in a field, shaking with dread.

He was so tired all the time, tired in his bones, tired in his head. The chemo was breaking him down, but it had the cancer at a stand still. He just needed a good sleep to help him get back on track.

But the good sleep never came. No nap was ever enough. He couldn't drink much anymore because it usually made him sicker. He wasn't smoking either. He became even grouchier and finally started to take it out on those around him. Then he felt horrendously guilty and never said he was sorry.

One day he finally had enough and told Mello to shut the hell up about the stupid Bust 'Em Down Barn!!!. Mello had stopped in at The Next Wave to say hello, and wouldn't stop talking about his new job, about how they flew the cheese for their pizza in from Italy or some crap and then John snapped at him in front of everyone, "What, do you jerk off to that place every night? Why don't you get a life and stop bothering everybody? Some of us have other things to think about." But John was just jealous because he felt he had no life. When he was at work he always wanted to go home, but home was lonely. His cats were sad. Martin wasn't the same, lately. Charlie was sad, and now even Aubrey seemed down. Mello would probably be sad for an hour or two, until he went to work.

John wanted to go visit Caroline. He wanted to say goodbye. He didn't belong here anymore.

29

"Spectacular, right? I told you guys it was cool." Mello waved his hand at the room triumphantly. "This is where I work- this bar right next to Slaughterhouse Lanes." He urgently motioned for everyone to follow again. "C'mon."

John looked around, trying to take it all in. The entire bowling alley in Bust 'Em Down Barn!!! was decorated to tell the story of a cow's journey from the pasture to the table. The wall that ran the length of the lanes was adorned with flashing neon bovines. Matching farmers with happy smiles and blue overalls gently patted them on the rear, and another neon sign of a red slaughterhouse with a conveyer belt depicted where they were all headed. Further down hung more signs of various cuts of meat and over the lanes were giant burgers, ribs, steaks, hotdogs, a basket of fries, and a picnic barbecue scene, all blinking frantically like an epileptic vegetarian's nightmare.

Aubrey, Charlie, and John followed Carmello further into the bowels of the barn, until they got to a large, open courtyard in the middle, which appeared to be a Chicken Coop themed mini-golf course. "Impressive," Aubrey said, nodding. It was his idea to go visit Mello at his new job. He invited them after work. John tried to get out of going, but caved in after pressure from Charlie and Old Jay.

"You're not going either," John had said to Jay.

"I'm too old for that crap."

"Me too."

"No, you're just sickly. It'll be good for you. If there's too many televisions on the wall, it gives me a headache. I have to drink in bars that have one TV, or better yet, a radio."

"It'll be fun," Charlie added, smiling wide between locks of curly brown hair. In a turnaround, he had been happy for more then a few days. He kept talking about doing things. He was charming and full of jokes and goofy behavior. "We'll check out all the waitresses. Mello says they have some hot ones, and the uniforms are kind of skimpy." John finally agreed because Charlie seemed so happy. It was infectious.

"You guys start some golf, then come over and bowl when you're ready. I've got to get back behind the bar." Mello reached into his shirt pocket and produced three small credit cards. "I got you guys each a card with forty dollars worth of games on it. That should keep you busy for awhile." Everyone took his card with thanks, even John, and Mello smiled proudly.

Bust 'Em Down Barn!!!'s allure was impossible to deny. It was shiny and new and everyone there was happy. John wasn't feeling too sick, only a little tired, so he started to have a good time too. Aubrey and Charlie didn't rush him along, which was nice. They played two games of golf that Charlie dominated, then slowly walked over to the bowling alley and drank a couple of beers while they waited for their lane to open. John needed to rest anyway. They got a light buzz on and were soon laughing and telling jokes. Mello started flipping bottles around like one of those trick bartenders from the movies and poured them a shot of whiskey. Then he snuck a couple of shots for himself.

139

John wasn't used to drinking anymore, but the warm feeling returned like an old friend. Jay was right. This was good for him. He was certainly feeling better.

A little hamburger-shaped pager buzzed to let them know their lane was ready.

They got up to go, but when John rose he saw white spots. His head spun as if it were tipping off his neck. He grabbed at the bar, or where he thought the bar should be, and ended up nearly groping some woman. She gasped and he mumbled a lame apology and slid to the floor with a numb thump.

He managed to grab hold of a chair and hoist himself back up. He instinctively turned to look for his friends, out of embarrassment, to see if they'd seen what happened. Mello was talking with someone at the end of the bar, and Aubrey and Charlie were already picking out balls, so John joined them. It was strange, but he was a little sad that no one had seen him fall except that lady. He wanted to go home.

He picked a lighter ball than he usually would, because he was so weak. Even getting that to hit the pins was a challenge. He couldn't stride up to the lane with any kind of authority or speed, most of his turns ended in the gutter, and his arm ached by the fourth frame. It was all a little disappointing. Still, he never complained or willingly let on that he was ready to be done. Charlie and Aubrey kept drinking, so John had a sip on his beer every five minutes to be polite. Slowly they got drunker, Charlie much more so than Aubrey, and John got more sleepy.

John must have fallen asleep in his chair, because out of nowhere he was waking up to Aubrey gently shaking his shoulder. "C'mon," Aubrey slurred quietly. "Mello's manager says you can't sleep here. We're done anyway, let's go."

"Ok. Sorry."

"Is fine."

John stopped in the bathroom and splashed cold water on his face to perk himself up. He wouldn't let Aubrey help him walk. He wasn't even drunk. Charlie was closer to needing help than John, but he was ahead of the group, waiting in the parking lot, grinning like a leprechaun.

As they were about to get in Aubrey's car, a loud voice boomed from several parking spaces away, "Get the fuck out of my car!"

Everyone turned and looked. So did other people in the lot.

It came again, "Get the fuck out of my car!"

John stood on his toes and saw a man bent down, two spaces over, addressing the driver's seat of a car. The window was down, the car was running, and he appeared to be yelling at no one. At first John thought maybe he'd caught someone stealing his car, or his buddy was drunk and trying to drive, but there was no one there. The guy sounded very angry. He just kept saying it over and over, and was getting louder.

"Get the fuck out of my car!" John peered around the truck to get a better look and saw there was indeed someone in the driver's seat. It was a very small and cowering woman. She was crying a little. The guy was Asian, with big glossy muscles and a tank top. She was just small. John couldn't tell any more than that. She may have been drunk. Maybe it was a lovers' quarrel. The guy didn't try to open the door, but he was getting louder. John looked around, wondering if anyone was going to do anything. Did something need to be done at all?

Just as that thought entered his mind, John saw Charlie Trout rounding the corner of the pickup, his hands clenched tight.

Charlie walked up and pushed the man square and fast, with locked wrists, nearly knocking him over.

"Why don't you back off, man?" Charlie was already in the guy's face, ready and wanting more.

"Fuck you, man. That's my girlfriend and my car. Mind your business."

"Take a walk, and talk to her later."

"You take a walk." The guy was bigger than Charlie, angry, and drunk. He shoved Charlie hard. Charlie came back with a punch squarely to his nose. At this the girl screamed and got out of the car, yelling for him to stop. Aubrey was instantly trying to pull him off. Aubrey was stronger than either of them, but Charlie was fast and breathing fire. He was on top of the Asian guy, punching with the same right jab, strong and fast, again and again. The guy wouldn't be conscious much longer, if he still was anymore. The girl was smacking Charlie and Aubrey with her purse, crying and asking them to please, please, please stop.

Aubrey finally got a bear hug around Charlie and lifted him and threw him about six or seven feet behind him. Charlie slid on his butt and rose, his face flush and his veins pulsing. Aubrey pointed a finger and said, "Stay back, Charlie." But Charlie tried to get around him, so Aubrey scooped him up like a linebacker and slammed him against his truck. He practically threw him into the cab. John got in next and put his hand on his leg. Charlie was crying. He didn't try and climb over John or go out the driver's side, for which John was grateful. Aubrey hopped in the front and put it in gear like a getaway professional and tore out of the parking lot.

The girl was helping her boyfriend up, his face bloody and cringing. A crowd of people had gathered.

Aubrey looked at Charlie. "I sure am pissed at you. But if I go to jail you're going to have to answer to my wife. That's worse than anything I could ever do to you."

142

30

John couldn't think of any advice to give Charlie, so he didn't say anything except goodnight when they dropped him off at Laura's house. He had wanted to say something, but he didn't have the words. As they got older, a lot of men seemed to feel it was their duty to dispense their own personal brand of wisdom on the younger generation. John never was that man. He didn't think he'd figured out enough, or if he had figured anything out at all, he figured it was only good enough knowledge for himself, what with every person being so uniquely blessed with their own hardships. It just didn't seem likely to do much good. Not to say that he looked down on men who casually threw the slim fruit of their life's lessons to the younger generation as if they were infallible and beyond criticism, but he did raise an eyebrow.

This time was different, though. He felt like he needed to tell Charlie something, even if it was just some bullshit he made up to make him feel better. But he couldn't think of anything. It was as if his mind were empty. He felt like one of those symbols, those snakes that fed on their own tail, and he was getting smaller and smaller.

It was still early when they dropped off Charlie. The sun hadn't been down more than an hour and a half. Aubrey told him to take the next day off if he needed it, and he looked like he needed it. He'd passed out multiple times on the ride home, bouncing back and forth between the two of them. He sputtered a fragmented apology of sorts as he slipped out of the truck, his breathing audible and drawn out, like a toddler's. It took him nearly three minutes to get the screen door open, but he made it home safe.

The next day Charlie didn't come to work, but there wasn't much to do. At lunchtime Aubrey opened the door to the office and said to John, "It's only eighty-five. Wanna eat lunch on the roof today?"

"Why, is that where we keep our food now?"

"No."

"I suppose you've got some kind of hippy garden up there, then? Some zen gook shit."

"Wow."

"Wow what, nancy?"

"That's the first time I've ever heard you use a racial slur."

"So?"

"So, you've quit jobs before because your boss told some black or Jew jokes. Walked out without a word, and never returned."

"That only happened twice."

"I guess it just seems out of character. You're an awfully principled man. Almost detrimentally so."

"What the hell do you know about principals? You want to eat on the roof."

"Nothing, I guess."

"It's true, I don't like that shit. But I thought I might give it a try."

"And?"

"I still don't like it, but I guess it's not so bad."

144

"You're crazy. Come on, let's eat on the roof. I've got sandwiches and stuff from home in the cooler."

They went around to the back of the workspace and Aubrey pulled down a fold out ladder from the ceiling.

"Are you kidding me? I can't be running up and down ladders all day."

"The view's wonderful."

"It can't be that much better than the ground."

John slowly climbed the ladder and found a latched entrance to the roof. He unlocked it and pushed, the hinges of the door loose and creaking. He emerged into bright sunlight and saw a couple of lawn chairs set up like a lonely outpost. Aubrey followed with a Coleman cooler.

"It's hotter than hell up here," John said. "I'm going back downstairs to spend the remaining moments of my existence in comfort."

"Hold on," Aubrey replied, and then went back down the ladder. He reappeared a moment later with a huge patio umbrella. "There's soda and beer in the cooler, help yourself."

John reluctantly grabbed a beer and Aubrey made another trip and returned with the umbrella's base, then with a heavy-duty work fan, and he set them up and placed the lawn chairs out of the sun. He flipped the latch to an outdoor power outlet which was mounted to the ledge of the building, plugged in the fan and turned it on.

"Alright, let's eat."

They ate some food and drank a little beer.

"I love it up here," Aubrey said, after a long silence punctuated only by chewing and staring at the vast space of rock, shrub and open sky before them. Past the fenced-in graveyard of cars, the land descended in a gradual slope for a good mile and a half southeast and then bowled out into a little valley. The view went for miles. "It's kind of my own little sanctuary."

"More like purgatory. None of this stuff helps with the heat enough to justify coming up here."

"This is the only place I can really think for an extended period of time without being interrupted."

"Then why'd you bring me up here?"

"I don't know." Aubrey looked at the sky.

"Well it is a good view," John conceded, although only slightly better than the one offered from the ground.

"Once when I was in high school I snuck up here to smoke a joint while Jay and my dad were working. I got stoned out of my gourd and watched a big wild storm come tearing across this basin here. You know the kind. You see it developing from so far off that it looks like some terrible monster."

"Yeah."

"That's the day I got the name for this place."

"I thought you named it after some dip-shit band you used to be in with that waste of space Carmello."

"I did, but I got the name for the band that day up here, watching the storm. Before it rained so hard on me that I had to run back downstairs. It only seemed natural that I'd give this place the same name, after I took over."

"I don't follow you."

"I was watching all that water falling out of the sky, and it just got me to thinking about the end, you know? Kind of like when the asteroid hit and wiped out the dinosaurs, the earthquakes and tsunamis, the ice caps melting. I pictured this enormous flood of water, like an entire sea coming toward me over all this land and rock. Like the next time it all happens. The Next Wave is the last one I'll ever see, you know?"

"No tsunamis of water is going to make it all the way to New Mexico."

"I know, but it was just a teenage stoner's daydream. You get the idea."

"Sounds morbid. Here all these years I thought the dumb name on that sign over there was something positive."

"It doesn't have to be something negative. It's not to me. Sure, I worry about it some, but there's also a part of me that finds it kind of comforting, that there's so much out of my control when it finally comes down to it. I don't have to worry about the big stuff. Only my dusty little corner of the world. The rest will take care of itself."

"Maybe you want to worry a little more, because if you haven't noticed, your dusty little corner of the world is dusty and hot, and full of things that would just as soon kill you as look at you. Being at the mercy of the universe isn't everything it's cracked up to be."

"Not much that can help it."

"Nope."

"Beer and a friend's all right."

"Yup."

They finished eating, John leaving half a sandwich. They packed everything and John eased himself slowly back down the ladder to finish his day of work, but before he did, he looked out again from the roof, at the shrubs and dirt, at the long slope downward and the little valley. Aubrey was right. You could almost see it coming.

31

In the midnight of his dreaming he felt no pain. It would happen for maybe an hour a night. Then it would pass and he'd drift in and out of nauseating waves until morning and wake up to face the wreckage that was his life.

Summer was now over and fall had sidled into place like a cold partner in bed.

If John had never gone to chemo, he would probably be dead now. He kept trying to remember why he was continuing. Beating it was a pipedream at this point. It seemed as though he was living only to suffer, yet some unseen force was driving him, not letting him give up. It certainly wasn't him, or at least nothing on the surface. A primal intelligence from someplace dark and old as time prodded him along, made him crawl on his fingernails through this bed of needles.

The wheelchair was hard to get used to, but he could no longer get around without it. He was one hundred and twenty-five pounds of weak, immobile flesh. He would slip out of bed and into his token of appreciation from the veterans' hospital and make his way to the bathroom. He'd usually take a bath, because he couldn't stand long enough to take a shower, and he only filled the tub up about six inches, because sometimes he couldn't get out right away and didn't want to drown. He laughed that he didn't want to drown. Forty-five minutes later he was usually ready to get up and do nothing. He couldn't work anymore. Aubrey had understood. It was only a charity job anyway. He'd feed his cats and eat some toast if he could keep it down, and drink some coffee.

Then he'd usually sit on the porch and ignore the mail, which was mostly bills he couldn't pay, and Martin would usually be there and lay his head in his lap. Sometimes Old Jay would walk over and eat his lunch with him and visit. On the days that he went to chemotherapy, Mello would pick him up and drive him there. Some nights Laura would bring soup. Occasionally Charlie would come too.

At night he would drink as much beer as his stomach would allow, which was sometimes none, and every now and then he'd take one drag of a Camel light before sleep. One night he drank more than usual and passed out on the porch. He woke up to violent shivers and Martin licking his hand fervently. After that he stopped drinking outside.

On the days that he wanted to go somewhere and didn't have any help, he would finagle his way out of the chair and sit next to it on the porch steps and then push it down the steps and watch it crash. Then he would slip his skinny butt down each stair until he was at the bottom and pull the chair upright and crawl back in. It was so hard to do that he only did it four times. Plus he broke the chair once and Mello had to lie and say he backed over it with his truck so they'd give him a new one.

Caroline was going to come and get him in two weeks. He was just waiting for that. They had talked on the phone and both agreed he couldn't stay at home anymore, but neither of them mentioned the reason he was going out to Minnesota was to die.

She was a grandmother now. Her daughter, Shannon, had the baby a month before. She named her Gracie. John could tell it made Caroline happy to have a grandbaby, and it made him feel lousy that his sorry ass was making her sad during this wonderful time in her life. Lousy time to die.

On the first day after he talked to Caroline on the phone about coming to stay with her family, he had a chemo treatment scheduled for mid-morning. He got up and got ready as he always did, and waited for Carmello to come barreling up the road to his house, late and scrambling, as was customary. But Mello was early this time, by five minutes.

"You had me worried for a second there," John said.

"What do you mean? I'm early."

"I know. I thought I'd died and gone to heaven, but then I realized heaven would have to be a lot better than just seeing your ugly ass arrive on time."

"That's funny. You expecting to get to heaven," Mello said, getting out of the truck and going up the steps to help John down.

"I do expect to get to heaven, because I've already done my time in hell, here on earth, just knowing you." John put his arm around him and leaned against him to keep from falling. After he got in the truck, panting and sweating, Mello went and got the chair, and with a lot of trouble, got it folded and loaded in back.

Halfway to the veterans' hospital Mello's cell phone rang. It was loud and annoying. John had heard it a thousand times. It was the theme song to *Rocky*, or something like that. Mello jerked around and nearly swerved off the road fishing it out of his front jean pocket. He flipped it open and John silently wished he wouldn't answer his phone while driving. "Hello?" he said, and then there was a long pause. "Yeah, I'm with John right now." John noticed a change in his voice, a tension, then a near panic. "Are you sure? Ok." Mello pulled the phone away from his mouth and looked at John. "It's Laura. She wants to talk to you."

"What about?" John asked, but Carmello just handed him the phone. "Laura? Are you alright?"

"It's Charlie." Her voice wheezed raspy from the phone. She sounded like she'd just run a thousand-yard dash. "John, he's going to kill him."

"What?"

"He's going to kill him and go to jail."

"Hold on. Kill who?"

"Bud White."

John remained strangely calm. "Where is he?" he asked.

"I don't know where Bud is, but Charlie thinks he does, and he's on his way to the Reynolds' old place out on county thirteen. He's got a gun. I saw it with his things when I was doing laundry last week, and I didn't say anything."

"Hold on. We just passed thirteen a few minutes ago. We can turn around."

"I know."

"Turn around, Mello. Go back to thirteen." John looked at him. "Do you know where a Reynolds' place is out here?"

"Yeah," Mello said, making a wide U-turn.

John brought the phone to his ear again. "Did you call nine-one-one?"

"The sheriff's at a conference somewhere, the deputy is sick, and the only state trooper in the area was on a call thirty miles away, but he's coming now."

"Where's Aubrey?"

"He's already on his way over there. He might beat you. He might even beat Charlie, I don't know."

"What happened? Is Bud really there?"

"I don't know. Jay was talking with some old guy at the pump and Charlie overheard him. The guy said he saw a light on in the top of the old barn when he was driving home last night. He thought it was odd and remembered that the sheriff's office had searched that property for Bud after Piper died, because he had a friend who owned it now. He was going to call the sheriff but forgot because he was tired when he got home. So he went to bed and remembered while he was talking to Jay. Charlie heard him and Jay said he took off."

"So Bud might not even be there. Some guy who's older than dirt thought he saw a light."

"What if Charlie hurts someone?"

"He'll probably get there and realize Bud isn't there and go home and get drunk and sleep it off. We'll make sure. We'll call you back in a couple of minutes."

"Please don't hang up."

"The damn thing is beeping at me because Mello never charges it, so I have to go. But I'll call you as soon as we find out he's ok."

"You promise?"

"Yes." They hung up and John dropped Mello's cell phone in the cup holder and said, "Get us there fast."

In about fifteen minutes they were roaring up a rock drive onto a property with an enormous and decrepit barn with peeling white paint. Various automobiles were parked or abandoned between it and an old house. Both Aubrey and Charlie's trucks were there, the door to Aubrey's hanging open.

"Oh my god," Mello gasped. "He's killed everyone."

"None of these people are dead," John said. But there were three men lying on the ground, slowly moving, holding their bloody heads from recent blows. A woman and another man stood away from the barn, closer to the house. They watched its slightly ajar door, frightened and enthralled. John didn't see Aubrey or Charlie.

As Mello stopped the engine they heard four gunshots crack like the sound of rams head-butting on a cold morning. They came from the barn as sure as they came from anywhere. Mello stared, his mouth open and panting. John slapped his leg. "Help me in there."

Mello opened the door and almost fell out of the truck. John waited anxiously while he started to go and get the wheelchair, but then he turned around and ran to John's door and opened it.

John put his arm around him. "C'mon. Help me." Mello did. He nearly lifted John out of the truck. They shuffled and limped like drunk partners in a three-legged race, passing the dazed men on the ground, then nearly fell over but kept going, all the while listening for more shots but hearing nothing.

They reached the barn door and stopped. They heard something now, a soft and pain-filled whimpering, like a dog.

They pushed aside the door and slid their feet across the straw and dirt. Aubrey's back was to them. He turned and looked at them. Past him was Charlie, pointing a pistol at a shifting dark shape in the corner. They went further into the barn and Aubrey held out his hand as if to say stay back. They came a little closer. Charlie was crying. Bud White writhed on the straw like a wounded snake, his legs shot up and leaking blood across the barn floor. He'd been crawling away for many feet, toward the back corner.

"Charlie, son," John said. "You got 'em. You can give me the gun now."

"I already told Aubrey I'm going to kill him. You can't stop me."

"Ok." John made Mello bring him closer, so they were standing next to Aubrey. Charlie didn't turn around. "We won't. Maybe you'll just let me talk to you before you do it."

"Nope." Charlie sniffed tears and snot back up his nose.

Bud White's face was empty of color and contorted in pain and fear when he looked back. He moaned, but said nothing. John felt there was a good chance he would pass out soon from blood loss and die anyway.

John watched Charlie carefully. His every muscle was taut and primed. His hand was steady, for the most part. He was crying harder. Suddenly he screamed at Bud, "Why'd you do it?" His cracking voice filled the old barn's rafters. Dust particles slowly floated like snow, illuminated in three long shafts of light from the open door and two windows. "Why?" Bud said nothing. "So help me, I'm gonna blow your fucking pecker off right now if you don't tell me why you killed her."

"I don't know." Bud managed, his voice squeaking.

Charlie walked up to Bud fast and put the gun to his shoe and pulled the trigger, blowing a smoking hole in his foot, and spraying blood and bone onto the floor beneath him. Bud screamed. Charlie took a step or two back and leveled the pistol at him again. "Tell me why you did it and I'll blow your head off. Or you can say nothing and loose your dick for the rest of your fucking life."

John let go of Mello and started to walk forward. Mello tried to hold on to him, but John pushed him away. He could barely stand. His legs felt like they were going to break underneath him.

"Charlie, give me that. This is enough."

"It's not right what he did," Charlie sobbed.

John reached him and put his hand on his shoulder, but not to steady himself. He still held himself up. "This
154

isn't about what's right. It's about you getting the best life you've got coming to you, after all this pain."

Charlie didn't move.

"I know it seems like this is all there is, but believe me, there will be more."

"This is all there is."

"There will be more."

"It's not fair."

"You won't find fairness in life. But you can find peace in yourself if you're willing to look for it." John hoped he wasn't lying. He hoped Charlie could find what he couldn't. "You're not like him. Trust me."

"He deserves to die."

"I'll kill him," John blurted out. "Gimme that goddamned thing."

Charlie turned a little and handed it over. John was so surprised that he almost dropped it. Bud's eyes followed them.

"Walk away right now," John said. Charlie took some steps away, and John heard Aubrey embrace him. John collapsed to the floor and felt something snap in his leg. He sat a foot or two from Bud White and pointed the gun at his face. It was so heavy. His finger twitched. He looked him in the eye. He wanted to know what was in him, but the sirens were coming and there wasn't time for a conversation, and Bud didn't look like he knew what he was anyway, so instead he told him, "Move and I'll kill you."

Bud must have believed him, because all he did for the next few minutes was breathe.

John tore a major ligament in his leg that he forgot as soon as he heard, and bruised his butt. They made him stay in the hospital for two days for observation and told him he'd need surgery or his leg would hurt for the rest of his life. He declined.

Laura came to visit him on the second night. She brought flowers

"John, I have some bad news."

"What could possibly dampen my mood now?"

"Martin was hit by a car. I found him behind the diner this morning when I got to work." A tear ran down her cheek. "He must have died in the night. Carmello and I buried him in your backyard. I hope that's ok."

"We were close this last year." John started to cry. "I guess I thought he'd always be around." He coughed.

"It's ok. You liked him. And he liked you, even though it took you a long time to reciprocate." She laughed and held his hand. She was warm.

"I did like him. He was my stinkiest friend, after Mello."

"I don't know why you wanna go see this guy," Mello said, pumping his brakes so he could stop in time to avoid rear-ending the car ahead.

"I don't know either," John admitted, trying to muster the energy for this excursion. His pants bunched around his thin waist uncomfortably as he sat in the passenger seat, his belt pulled to the last hole. "Guess I just wanna know a couple of things."

"I think it's stupid. He's not gonna want to see you, anyway."

"I saved his life. I bet he'll see me."

They finally pulled up to the hospital but Mello couldn't find a close spot, so they had to park far away. Mello came around after he got the wheelchair from the back and helped John into it. He pushed John to the hospital entrance and they headed toward the front desk.

"If he's not hear I'm done looking for the day," Mello said. "Three hospitals in one day just to talk to some low life piece of..." He stopped as they rolled up to the desk. John asked if they had a Bud White and the woman replied they did, but that his visits were restricted.

"It's ok, they're expecting us. I'm his uncle and this his mongrel cousin."

"He's in six fifty-eight, but the police may not let you in."

"I'm sure they will. Thank you."

"Are you crazy?" Mello said lowly as he pushed John to the elevators.

"Just let me talk."

"Sure." Mello breathed a sigh of relief when they got to the elevator and there was no one in it. "These places really creep me out."

"You won't get sick," John said, putting his arm in front of the door to hold it for someone, which then turned into another four people crowding in. Mello quietly squealed in frustration.

They got out on the sixth floor and went to the room with the policeman sitting outside. The officer looked up from his hunting magazine. He looked bored and annoyed.

"I'm here to see Bud White. Is he available?"

"Depends. Are you family or his lawyer?"

"No sir."

"Friend?"

"I'd hesitate to use that word."

"Then the answer's no."

"Tell him I saved his life. I bet he'll see me, if for no other reason than curiosity."

The officer looked put out, but he got up, knocked lightly on the door and entered the room. He was gone for about a minute. When he came out he pointed at John and said, "You can go in. Judas Priest has to stay."

"I don't wanna go anyway."

"You have five minutes, but if he asks you to leave sooner, you have to go." He held the door open for John, but he couldn't see anything inside.

"Ok, thank you." John wheeled himself awkwardly into the room, as he wasn't good at maneuvering on his own, and saw Bud White's face, swollen and purple from

158

being beaten. He looked heavily sedated. His legs were covered. Tubes of precious liquids went in and out of him and it looked like he had a catheter.

"What do you want?" he croaked.

"How're your legs feeling?"

"I may never walk again. What does that tell you?"

"Right."

"I asked what you wanted."

John stopped at the end of the bed, suddenly very weary. "I guess I just wanted to see you. I honestly don't know why."

Bud laughed. "So now you seen me. You want me to thank you?"

"No. I almost killed you myself, I don't want thanks."

"Why didn't you?"

"I don't know. I guess I've killed enough people."

"Whoopdeefrickindoo." Bud snorted something out of his swollen nasal passages and hocked a big bloody wad onto the floor. "You should have let her pussy-ass boyfriend kill me. He's gonna regret not doing it for the rest of his life."

"Maybe. But you'll regret it more when you get to prison with that pretty face and a couple of legs that don't work so good."

Bud's face dropped. His eyes went dark.

"Why'd you get kicked out of the military?" John asked.

"What?"

"You heard me." John wheeled himself just a little closer.

"What difference does it make?"

"It doesn't I guess. You here all the stories about you?"

"They ain't true."

"No?"

"No. I never raped anyone before. Before her. Except there was this girl in middle school, but she was just drunk and forgot she wanted it right when we were starting, so I just finished. But that doesn't count, cause she didn't even remember after."

"Whatever you say."

"I loved Piper. I didn't mean for what happened to happen."

"Thought you'd say that."

"I'm serious. I loved her."

"Then why did it happen?"

"I don't know. Because she didn't want me any more." His face seemed to plead for a moment. He looked away. "I always knew I wadn't right. I don't know why."

"You really messed up. With your priors, they're gonna put you away for the rest of your life."

"You can go now. Wheel your ass outta here."

"Alright." John turned his chair around and accidentally bumped into the bed. Bud winced. "Sorry," he said.

Just before he got to the door, Bud said, "There was this boy, a Sunni kid." John stopped and waited. He didn't look at him at first, but then he did and saw that Bud wasn't looking at him either. His face was half covered in shadow, staring at a sliver of light on the floor from the closed window. "He used to throw rocks at our convoy every day when we drove past. For about three months. One day we got the idea to grab him and drop him off in a Shiite neighborhood about twenty miles away. Just to teach him a lesson. We roughed him up a little. Dropped him off. He stopped throwing rocks. We thought he'd settled down. He never made it back, I guess. Two

160

months later, one of his uncles or cousins who seen us grab him identified me and another guy, made a big stink about it. We got honorably discharged." He didn't appear as if he was going to say anything else, and John thought he was finished. Then he added, "Tell one of those nurses out there to bring me a popsicle. They put me in a room with a buzzer that only works half the time." He nodded.

John nodded too and wheeled himself out of the room and Mello took over pushing him down the hall.

"You get what you wanted?"

John shrugged and it hurt to move and he said, "I guess. Pretty much what I thought."

"Which is?"

"He definitely likes popsicles."

34

Charlie was arrested for assaulting Bud White and released on bail. It didn't look like he'd end up doing any time. His defense attorney said that since he didn't kill him, the prosecutor was going to be hard pressed to convince a jury that Charlie was anything other than a hero. He went back to work right away.

Two weeks after Mello took him to see Bud White in the hospital, Caroline and her husband came to take John to Minnesota. Her husband was named Randall. He was a nice man, for being so inconvenienced by someone he'd never met. John tried to tell some jokes to lighten the mood, and they laughed, but he knew they'd fallen flat, and it made him sad. There wasn't much that could brighten things.

They rented a minivan to accommodate his wheelchair and the carrying cases for his two cats. He packed very little. What did one pack to go die? You needed some supplies, obviously, but not too many. He found it rather difficult, but after packing minimal toiletries and cat food, ultimately settled on seven pair of underwear, four pair of socks, four undershirts, three nice flannels, one pair of shoes and a jacket. He was all out of money, so he hoped he'd die before Caroline had to buy him anything. It was already too much that she was going to have to go back and settle his estate later.

Before he left, John looked at every room in his house one last time. He originally planned to ask Caroline and Randall to drive him around and say goodbye to his friends, but decided not to after his jokes didn't work out. What was there to say? He looked out the window as they drove past The Next Wave. Old Jay was sitting in a lawn chair in front like a stone sculpture with red overalls. Although Jay didn't see him, John felt guilty as they passed by, like he was making a break for it. But that was always how he left places. He never said goodbye, and never looked back.

He suddenly thought about how lonely his life had been because of this. He thought of the casual friends he'd left behind over the years, but there weren't many. He could hardly think of anyone other than his most recent acquaintances.

He thought about Martin, and how he'd lurched over to Laura's Diner after being mauled by that car, searching for a place that was friendly, where he knew he could get help and be safe.

35

The drive was uncomfortable, but that was to be expected. Bathroom stops were especially unnerving. Randall initially offered to help John, but John was not about to have that. He could still sort of stand up and move, although with his injured leg, it hurt so bad he cried.

He felt like he had a duty to be somewhat of a conversationalist and make them feel comfortable around him, so he talked some, but the ride made him sleepy. The country flashed by his window in a panoramic blur.

He dreamed his life being projected onto the window, whizzing forward through all the happy times, and the sad, the embarrassments, the warmth from his mother when she held him when he was young, how much he missed her when she was gone, he the only child old enough to have memories of her, passing on his few recollections to sad young eyes, hungry for her contact, his first ride on a bike, the time his father whipped his ass raw for cussing at the dinner table, the few times he could remember not being at odds with the old man, their rolling fistfight on the kitchen floor, the time he lost his virginity to Diana Hindquist in the middle of the night on the grass in her backyard, his time in Vietnam, a flash of faces, happy, smiling comrades, then dead friends, and nameless dead enemies calling out, demanding to be recognized, the many towns he went through, the booze, the nightmares, the uncontrollable rage, the handful of girlfriends and one night stands, the fights that cost him their love and affection every time, Laura and his last years in Entierro, and every misstep there, and there were many, until he was finally sitting in that minivan, on that highway, crumbling and soft and fading away.

36

Minnesota would have seemed nicer, under different circumstances. Autumn there was cool and crisp, and the leaves burst forth in the final bloom. But soon enough the rains materialized to claim their due, and the leaves abandoned their former dwellings to brown and decay, bunching together in the gutters like soppy oatmeal.

Caroline set up a bed for him in their basement office and the cats had the run of the floor since their kids were grown, which wasn't so bad. Luckily, Merlin chose to attack only John in response to his sudden and catastrophic change in living conditions, and John had long ago mastered the art of deflection with a stiff kick of the shin, or sweeping yet non-lethal block with the elbow. He could still execute these maneuvers from his wheelchair, and even became somewhat adept at turning it quickly so Merlin would latch onto a wheel instead of his leg. He worried, though, about how he would do when John was gone. There was a good chance they would have to put him down to avoid being sued.

They all watched some old movies together. That was actually the time when he felt most comfortable. He loved showing off his knowledge of the classics. Even John couldn't fail to bond with newly connected family members when Bogey and Gable and Hayworth and Hepburn were around to help. They ate popcorn and stayed up late some nights. John had fun with that, and liked to have a beer or two with Randall and shoot the breeze, but his health was always keeping it from getting too fun. He would get tired or start feeling too sick. It was embarrassing. Then Carrie would feel the need to hang around before he went to sleep and fuss over him like a little kid. This bothered him at first, but he came to secretly enjoy it.

After they'd gone upstairs to bed, sometimes John would imagine that he ended up marrying Laura, and they were visiting Caroline and Randall on vacation, and having a great time as a family, and he wasn't sick. Sometimes he would get ashamed if the fantasy was too detailed, but after a few nights he'd usually think about it again, and wish that he could wake up just one morning and live a day of that life.

37

No matter how they tried to make him feel at home, or how he tried to remember to enjoy his time as much as he could because these were his last days, he couldn't shake the feeling that he was a burden on Carrie. He knew she wouldn't have it any other way, and Randall was always nice to him and volunteered to take him outside for walks, but he still felt awkward. There was no dignity.

But he liked the walks, and he was getting weaker. He could do less and had to sleep more. So he let Carrie help him get bundled up and she and Randall would push him around their neighborhood until it got dark. They lived in a slightly rural suburb of Minneapolis, and saw deer and even a fox once, darting through the woods on the side of the road like phantoms.

John even got to meet Carrie's kids and the baby, Gracie. They all went out to eat at some old-fashioned burger joint. It reminded John of Laura's which made him homesick. It was nice getting to meet everyone, but there was something so formal about it, these young people all showing up to meet him since he wouldn't be around to know before too long. There was Carrie's daughter Shannon, her baby, Gracie, and her husband Gary, and her other daughter Phoebe, who was only just out of college and still shy and distant. Her son, Matt, was living out of state. California, John thought he heard her say. He was struck by the fact that he would never get to know anything more about these people than what he was learning now. He imagined that this one or that one shared this or that genetic trait with him, but he'd never know for sure.

What he liked the most was getting to see baby Gracie. She fascinated him. He hadn't been this close to a baby since he was a kid. She was so small, only eight weeks old, with wispy hair and blue eyes. John had blue eyes too. That was a definable trait they shared. He didn't think anyone else there had blue eyes, and then he remembered he had inherited his from his father.

He watched Gracie's petite hands grasping at the air, her eyes so innocent and beautifully vacant with youth. He imagined her growing up, never knowing her grandfather, never knowing her great-uncle John. He imagined her becoming a little lady and getting upset at all her little problems, which would seem so huge and real to her, and he thought it was lovely.

38

That night after they got home, as he was trying to get out of his wheelchair and into bed, John made a horrible discovery. He'd soiled himself. It must have happened moments before, because it stank so awful that there was no way it could have been there long. He hadn't felt the need to go. He pushed himself up and felt the chair. It had gone through and it was messy. His emotions ran almost instantly from shock to rage, and then a deep sadness. He wished he had a gun in his room. If he did, he probably would have ended his life without another thought.

He rolled out of his room and into the bathroom without knowing what he was going to do. His eyes scanned for a medicine cabinet, but there wasn't one in the basement. There was a shower with a small seat that he'd been using, but that still left the issue of what to do with his clothes, and he didn't think he could get in the bath without help. For the past few days, Carrie had to give him a hand. He wore a towel around his bony waist until she left the bathroom and wrapped up again and called for her when he was finished.

He looked around the basement, really wanting to find a way to end it, but that would mean he'd be leaving Caroline and Randy with an even bigger mess than the one he was currently sitting in. But on the plus side, they could call the ambulance to take him away and let the coroner clean him up. All they'd have to deal with was the emotional baggage, and would it really be any worse for them than it already was? Everything seemed to point towards taking charge of it himself.

But this didn't change the fact that he couldn't find anything to do it with and he was still sitting in filthy drawers. He went back to the bathroom and opened the closet behind the treadmill and pulled a string to turn on the light. He didn't see anything but some old weights and a gym bag, some clothes hanging, and an extra bag of cat food.

Just as he was about to call Caroline for help, he reached down and hooked the gym bag's strap with a finger and pulled it up. He unzipped all the pockets and pouches and pulled out an eighty-count bottle of generic acetaminophen. Would a bottle like this do it? Maybe not for a healthy person, but he was pretty sick. He looked at the white plastic bottle like it was an archaeological find and studied its directions and warnings and uses as if they were a bible.

He put it in his lap and turned around in his chair and rolled it to the sink. It felt so heavy, as if he were doing it under a couple of miles of water, thousands of pounds of pressure pushing down on all sides. He looked for his cats but didn't see them and contemplated going to find them to say goodbye, but he'd have time for that, and he was afraid of loosing his nerve if he didn't do it right away, so he tried three times and finally got the child-proof cap off and thought he was going to break his fingernail puncturing the paper seal. He dumped the bottle's contents into his lap and turned on the faucet. He took the pills a few at a time, cupping water with his hand and bringing it to his mouth to drink.

When the bottle was gone, he went into the family area of the basement and found Pirouette sleeping on the couch. He picked her up and she squawked a little, but stayed in his lap. He looked for Merlin, but couldn't find him. Then he started to panic. He had to find Merlin. He wanted to hold the prickly little bugger just one last time. Finally he found him asleep on the window ledge of the walk out sunroom, but when he picked him up, he scratched at John and freaked Pirouette out and they both ran away. He was left sitting in the basement's walkout sunroom, looking into the lower area of the backyard, at an empty concrete birdbath and the dark of night.

39

John's attempt on his own life was unsuccessful and this pissed him off greatly. After he had passed out, Caroline came down to get her day planner so she could work on some kind of party for a friend, and she found him too early and called 9-1-1.

He spent two days in the hospital and then was home for a few days before she brought him to an old folks home. She asked him why he did it and he said he was tired of people having to clean up after him. He was ready to go. As much as he hated being put in a home, he agreed with Caroline when she said she couldn't take care of him anymore. It was the best thing for everyone.

He just wished he'd been successful in speeding up the process. The longer he lived, the more money it was costing his sister and her husband, and this really aggravated him. At least he'd stopped all his chemo treatments after he got to Minnesota. It couldn't be too much longer. Maybe a few weeks in the home would do it. He could deal with that. He had a small refrigerator in his room and Randall brought him beer as a treat and he managed to talk him into smuggling in a carton of cigarettes. He drank a beer before bed if he could and wheeled himself outside to smoke a couple of times a day, which really bothered the caretaker staff. They told him he shouldn't smoke because he was sick. They shook their heads. He watched *Nick at Night* and *TV Land* until the nurses made him turn it off. If he was going out it was going to be a party.

He got a staph infection about two weeks after entering the home and within another week developed pneumonia. The H1N1 pandemic was happening and Dr. Cheepak, his physician, thought he had contracted that too. There were three other confirmed cases in the facility. He was on full time oxygen and couldn't leave his bed. The H1N1 brought on double pneumonia and he started seeing things. He saw three people in grey robes in the corner of his room, kneeling and praying beneath a hovering, glowing blue ball that shot lightning. He called the nurses and asked them to please remove them. "I don't want any part of that," he said. He saw Dale Podobinski in full army fatigues and a helmet, bringing him a shiny metal bucket to poop in.

"Doesn't matter how shiny the receptacle," John said.

"You were expecting something else?" Dale asked, inquisitively.

"No, bring it in. I just thought you'd understand, is all. I guess I was wrong."

"I do understand. It's you that doesn't."

"Oh, ok. My mistake. Have a nice day."

"You too," Dale said, and put the shiny metal bucket on John's chest and walked out of the room.

John tipped it and looked in and saw a bunch of tiny frogs floating in muddy water. "Oh that's ok," he said. "I could be a pile of frogs, I guess."

Soon enough everything went dark, and he couldn't remember how long it had been that way, but he could still hear people shuffling around him, hear their small voices as if they were on a floor above him in a house.

40

After he went into a coma, Caroline stayed with John eight hours a day and only went home to sleep. Randall was there as often as he could get away from the office. He was raised Catholic, and didn't really go to mass anymore, but one night he read John his last rights. He liked John, and wished he'd been able to know him better. Caroline said he had a really big heart, and he thought so too, in the short time he'd been around him. They were both very sad for him, and hoped it would end quickly, because he'd been suffering for so long.

Four nights passed and John was stable. He'd moan sometimes, or shuffle a bit. His fever was high and he wouldn't eat, but Caroline was able to put ice chips in his mouth. On the fifth night he seemed almost like he might come out of it. When she held the cup of ice to his mouth, her big brother would take more and more. His mouth would be full of ice and dripping water down his chin where it pooled on his chest. She dabbed it with paper towels.

"Honey, I know you're thirsty, but only take a few chips, you don't wanna choke." She held his hand and rubbed it.

"Gimme the whole damn cup," he suddenly mumbled, and then silence.

She tried to get him to talk again, but he now barely moved at all. She slowly gave him the rest of the ice, then went home and got a call from the hospital. He'd just died, they said, probably before she left the parking lot.

41

Caroline planned a small funeral for five days from his death. He had wanted to be cremated, but said she could bury his ashes or throw them into the street for all he cared. She was able to find his friend Carmello's phone number in her desk, still there from when he'd called her about John. She called him, but there was no answer, so she left a message explaining John's passing, and included the details of the funeral, but implied she didn't expect him to come. She just wanted him to know when it would be, so that maybe he and John's other friends could think of him that day. She wasn't surprised when she didn't hear back from him.

She arranged for military honors, which was offered free of charge by the government.

Two of her closest friends came with their husbands, as well as her daughters, Phoebe and Shannon, and Shannon's family.

It was late autumn, and winter's long tongue had licked all the trees bare. They stood craggy and silent. Everyone was outside at the cemetery, with five old veterans in uniform, the youngest not a day under eighty-five. Two of them sat on a bench near the casket, and the other three were a little further away with their rifles. Caroline stood and cried a little, not able to help it. She wrapped her sweater and scarf tight around her body, and

Randall held her hand. Her daughters took turns consoling her.

They were only waiting on the priest, who was late.

"Here comes someone, mom," Phoebe said.

They all turned and looked to see two men approaching nervously, one rather round with curly hair, a big beard, and coke bottle glasses that made his eyes look huge, the other one skinny, with long, greasy hair combed back and tucked behind his ears. The big one wore old but neatly ironed khakis and an ironed flannel shirt, tucked in, and the skinny one had on a dress shirt that was about four sizes too big and so full of starch that it looked as tough as a suit of armor. He wore jeans that were threadbare, and his shirt was open about five buttons, revealing an undershirt with a heavy metal emblem.

The big one spoke first. "Hello, Caroline. I'm not sure if you remember me. I'm Aubrey, John's friend." He held out his hand.

"Oh, of course, I'm sorry," she said, shaking his hand. "It's been quite the day."

"Sorry we're late," Carmello said, wiping his hand on his jeans before sticking it out. "We got a little lost trying to find the cemetery. It's our first time here."

"That's ok. We're still waiting to see if the priest is going to show up."

Everyone made introductions, and just as they finished, a man with a fuzzy mustache and no hair came walking down the hill. "Hello," he said. "I'm Father Henry." Father Henry apologized for being late. His last funeral had run over, and he had another one to do later in Blaine, but he had plenty of time for this one, and told them not to worry. He was efficient and quick to smile and repeat a name after it was given to him. He said they would start soon, but wanted to know a little about this man they were about to bury.

"He obviously served his country," Father Henry said, motioning to the veterans standing about.

"Yes he did," Caroline said. "He served bravely in Vietnam."

"Anything else, about his service, or maybe about his character, that you would like me to focus on?"

Everyone stood silent, and then Carmello blurted out, "He was a really good guy. He always looked out for the underdog. One time he quit a job because his boss told a racist joke. He just walked out without saying a word and never went back."

"So he was a man of principles?" asked Father Henry.

"Yeah," replied Aubrey, and Carmello nodded too. "Definitely a man of principles."

"Wonderful, then…"

Carmello cut him off, adding "Yeah, hell, just recently he kept one of our good friends from killing another guy. He was a hero. A stand up dude."

"Well that's very good," Father Henry said, looking uncomfortable.

It looked to Caroline like even Aubrey was squirming.

"Well then I'll guess we'll begin."

Father Henry gave a short eulogy about John, his service to his country, his principled life, and the wonderful people who loved him that he left behind. He was efficient and smiled warmly at everyone. The three veterans with the rifles pointed them into the air in unison and each fired three blank rounds at the sky. Taps played from somewhere, but it sounded like it came from a portable stereo and not a real person. The other two folded the American flag into a little triangle and one of them gave it to Caroline, who couldn't stop the tears from pouring out of her. The only person crying nearly as hard was Carmello.

As the old man handed her the flag, his hand shook and he said, "It is my pleasure to offer you this flag, on behalf of a grateful nation."

"What a load of malarkey," Mello said, breaking the silence as he and Aubrey walked down the slightly damp path of the cemetery.

"What do you mean?" Aubrey asked.

"That stupid priest didn't even give a damn. All he wanted to do was get out so he could have a beer and watch the game." Mello's eyes were still teary and red. He sniffed.

"He was a little fast. But you can't expect him to care too much. He probably does this kind of thing all the time."

"Those old farts with the rifle and the flag cared. You could see it all over their faces. And they do this thing all the time."

"Yeah. They did seem like they really cared."

"Damn right. John deserves better than a priest that doesn't care."

"You're right. But his sister cared. And her family. That's enough people for a good funeral. It doesn't have to be all flashy and everything. John probably wouldn't have liked that anyway."

"And we care too."

"Yeah. We care too." Aubrey patted him on the back.

The two old friends walked together out of the graveyard to Aubrey's truck and got in. Mello fiddled with the radio and complained that he couldn't find any good stations. He turned it off. Aubrey leisurely drove down the streets covered in dead leaves in this part of the country they didn't know and got on the highway to go home. At first they both were quiet.

Then Mello said, "Do you think John regretted not doing it?"

"Not doing what?"

"Not killing him."

"Who? Bud?"

"Yeah. He had the chance, but he didn't. He said he was going to, and if he said he was going to do something, he almost always did it."

Aubrey rubbed his fingers across the steering wheel as if he were feeling velvet. "I don't know. Maybe. I think letting him live was the right thing, but who knows? Sometimes it seems like everything is just a mistake."

"Yeah. But it's not, right?"

"I hope not. Not everything."

They were silent again for a long time. It was getting dark, just coming out of the grey hour and into the time when everything is draped in the thickness of night. They drove into what was coming because there wasn't anything else for them to do. After awhile they started talking again, and they slowly found their old rhythm, and their mood lightened some. They started telling stories about old times and the friend they'd just buried. They laughed a little and rolled the windows down a crack to feel the cool air from outside, which came in hissing, drowning out their voices, so they had to yell.